THE SILVER BOULDER

ADVENTURE • NET
#2

THE SILVER BOULDER

Andrea and David Spalding

Whitecap Books
Toronto/Vancouver

Edited by Lori Burwash
Proofread by Elizabeth McLean
Cover design by Susan Greenshields
Interior design by Antonia Banyard
Typeset by Graham Sheard
Printed in Canada

Canadian Cataloguing in Publication Data

Spalding, Andrea.
    The silver boulder

    (Adventure.net ; #2)
    ISBN 1-55285-105-2

    1. Kaslo (B.C.)—History—Juvenile fiction. I. Spalding, David A.E., 1937–
II. Title. III. Series: Adventure.net; #2
PS8587.P213S54 2000   jC813'.54   C00-910935-8
PZ7.S7334Si 2000

The publisher acknowledges the support of the Canada Council for the Arts
and the Cultural Services Branch of the Government of British Columbia for
our publishing program. We acknowledge the financial support of the
Government of Canada through the Book Industry Development Program for
our publishing activities.

For Jon, Rika, Morgan, and Bevan
— who introduced us to the Kootenays

ACKNOWLEDGMENTS

We would like to thank those who aided in our research, particularly our travelling companion and reality check, Rosalyn Rosher. We were privileged to interview Captain Adolph Osis, a former captain of the *Moyie*, and Nobby Hayashi of the Nikkei Internment Memorial Centre in New Denver. Beth Weathers of the Kootenay Lake Historical Society read the story for accuracy and told us about the *Moyie*'s real ghost. Paula Jamieson and Yoshiyuki Moriyama helped us with the Japanese language. Our daughters Penny Spalding and Jane Spalding-Jamieson read and criticized drafts and shared their childhood reminiscences of visits to the area. Our son-in-law Jock Mardres has provided invaluable help in locating and assessing suitable Web sites (as well as constructing ours).

No book appears without extensive work behind the scenes, and we appreciate the efforts of our indefatigable editor, Lori Burwash.

CHAPTER ONE

Tick...tick...tickaticka...tick...tickatickatickaticka. The
strange mechanical sound burst into a frenzy of clicking,
then fell silent.

Rick Forster opened his eyes and sleepily focused on
the crack of early morning sunlight at the edge of his
window blind. *Hmm, morning.* He stretched and let his
eyes wander around his tiny bedroom. It was set up like
a ship's cabin. Everything he needed neatly fitted into the
small space. However, the drawers beneath his bunk bed
were half open, with clothes tumbling out, and his desk
and computer were piled high with sheets of paper. The
tiny room looked disastrous. Rick sighed, "Gotta clean up.
Mom will have a fit." He closed his eyes again.

A few seconds later his eyes reopened. He focused
on the ceiling and sleepily scanned his posters. They
were plastered everywhere, his favourite bands, the last
Star Wars movie, pictures of dinosaurs, and—his latest
interest—a poster from an exhibit of crystals that glowed
in the dark.

Minerals! That clued him in. They were in Kaslo, B.C., a tiny mining village beside Kootenay Lake. It was dark when his dad drove the bus in last night, so Rick hadn't really seen it yet, but...

Ticka...tick...ticktickatick. The sound started again. TICKA TICKA TICKA TICKA... It became frantically insistent.

"Hey, that's what woke me up." Rick knelt on his bed and lifted the blind.

At the bottom of some steps leading to a beach, a young man with long hair and a red bandanna tied across his forehead was waving a long-handled stick with a disk on the end over the sand.

"Excellent!" Rick tumbled out of bed. He grabbed the nearest pair of jeans, pulled a T-shirt over his head, and flattened his brown cowlick with his hand. Rushing through the sleeping quarters of the bus, he banged on his sister's door as he passed.

"Wake up, Willow. It's morning. There's a guy outside with a metal detector. I bet he's looking for gold."

Rick leapt from the big blue converted school bus and raced down the steps to the beach.

The man was concentrating. He'd marked out large squares in the sand and was systematically sweeping a section at a time with the detector.

"Found anything?" asked Rick eagerly.

The man glanced up, but the clicking intensified. He swung the hub of the detector over the same spot several times. Switching it off, he hunkered down and sifted through the sand. He held up a couple of pennies to show Rick before dropping them into a soft leather bag tied to his belt loop.

"That's all?" said Rick with disappointment. "I thought you were looking for gold."

The man grinned. "Well, you never know," he said in a soft drawl. "A few cents here…a gold ring there. Some days I get a good haul. But if you're after real gold?" He shrugged. "Not much of that around here."

"There isn't?" Rick's shoulders drooped. "Dad said this used to be a mining area. I wanted to pan for gold."

The man chuckled. "Silver's more like it, and it's pick and shovel work. Silver, lead, and zinc. The mountains around here are riddled with 'em." He gestured towards the mountains towering behind the town. "The Silvery Slocan, that's what folks call this area. It's full of mines, and tales of lucky strikes. Lots of people dreamed of getting rich from those mountains, including me. But in Kaslo now, the only silver you'll find here is on the beach." He restarted the metal detector and began sweeping the next square.

"You're a miner? You search for silver, in the mountains?" Rick couldn't believe his luck.

"Guess you'd call me a prospector. I haven't found what I'm looking for yet. But one day I will." The man straightened up and his eyes flashed. "I'll find my grandfather's silver boulder, then my luck will be in." He jerked the bag at his belt. "This will be small potatoes."

11

The first Silver Boulder

 In 1892, miner Jim Cockle was pitching his tent in a valley in the Selkirk Mountains. He was cutting tent poles when he struck a rock with his axe, and was rewarded by a flash of metallic ore. The area was staked for a mine, but the discovery was not a seam that led into the mountainside, just a boulder—what miners call "float."

The rock had tumbled down from an ore deposit above, and was around the size of a mini-van, over 2 metres high and 3 metres wide. It was estimated to weigh 125 tonnes, and was composed mainly of galena, a shiny lead ore.

The miners were thrilled to sell the boulder for $2000, a small fortune in those days. The American buyer, W. D. Middaugh, broke it up and shipped it to a smelter. There he discovered that the galena contained an impurity worth more than the lead. The boulder was riddled with silver, and Mr. Middaugh received $20,000.

News of this silver boulder — the biggest ever found — travelled around the world and brought thousands of miners to the area. The town of Sandon grew up near the site of the discovery. Ever since, hopeful prospectors have been looking for another boulder like it.

"Wow, your grandfather really found a silver boulder?"

"I'm betting on it." The man's face hardened with determination. "Pure silver, my grandfather said, and nearly as high as a man. And I'll find it—even if I have to spend my live-long days looking in every darned gully."

Rick was speechless. A boulder of pure silver! Wait until Willow heard this!

CHAPTER TWO

Willow Forster wriggled into her jeans, opened her cupboard, and surveyed the neatly hung T-shirts. Pulling on her new crop top, she admired herself in the mirror. Her room was gloomy. She leaned over her bed, jerked the blind cord, and peered out the window.

They were parked on the sunny main street of a small village. "It's like a movie set, a western…all old wooden buildings," she murmured to herself.

Willow watched two elderly men slowly walk down the sidewalk and into a small café. Maybe everyone in the village was old. No. A smartly dressed young woman with a swinging bob of shiny black hair strode around the corner and also entered the café.

Willow's stomach rumbled. It was definitely breakfast time. She grabbed her hairbrush and walked through to the galley kitchen to fill the kettle and set it on the propane stove.

Wow! Kootenay Lake, backed by high snow-covered peaks, spread before her. She looked up the shoreline.

Kaslo in the Kootenays

 Long, narrow Kootenay Lake lies between forested slopes of snowy mountains. In 1889, settlers founded the community of Kaslo on its west shore. Only four years later, Kaslo was a city of 3000 people. Steamboats brought in prospectors and entrepreneurs, drawn by the rich mineral area in the Slocan Ranges to the west. The town was so busy that every hotel bed was booked in shifts so that three men could share it in a day.

In 1894, fire and flood almost destroyed the community, but Kaslo was quickly rebuilt. By 1895, the Kaslo & Slocan Railway reached into the mountains, carrying in supplies and bringing back ore. In Kaslo, 250 tonnes of ore were concentrated every day and shipped away by steamer.

Soon another railway reached into the mountains from the west, taking some of the traffic away from Kaslo. As mineral prices dropped, many mines closed. Kaslo turned to fruit growing, and cherry trees were planted everywhere— even along the streets.

Today, Kaslo's industries are logging, fruit, and tourism.

www.kaslo.com
www.bcadventure.com/adventure/explore/kootenays/
central.html

An old-fashioned sternwheeler was moored by the wharf. Cool.

Willow sat in the driver's seat, brushing and braiding her long fair hair and enjoying the sunny panorama. This trip was going to be different—she and Rick were not going to be shipped to summer camp while their parents worked. That was last summer. This summer her parents would be on call in Kaslo, and she and Rick would be allowed to hang out on their own. She grinned at her reflection in the driver's mirror. Could be fun.

Rick watched fascinated as the man swept the detector across another patch of sand, locating a wristwatch and more change. "Do you find lots of money?"

"Sometimes, in July and August. When the tourists line up to see the old *Moyie*." The man walked over to another square.

Rick followed. "What's the Mo...the mo-yay?"

"The *Moyie*." Seeing that Rick still looked baffled, the man repeated the word slowly. "The mo-yay—the old sternwheeler, up the shore." He pointed, then looked curiously at Rick. "Most folks visit Kaslo to see it."

"We're here with Mom and Dad. They're teaching film making. At the summer school," Rick said absently as he looked along the shoreline.

Beached beside the lake was a beautifully restored old sternwheeler. "Wow, I didn't know *that* was here!" Rick exclaimed. "Is it a real one? Can we go on board?"

The man laughed. "She's real, all right. Plied her way up and down Kootenay Lake for nearly sixty years. Lots of the older people in town have travelled on her. Yup. A lot of history on that sternwheeler. She'll open at nine-thirty. You have to pay though. She's a museum now."

A piercing whistle made them jump. They swung around to see Willow standing at the top of the beach steps, two fingers still in her mouth.

Rick waved and yelled, "Come down!"

He turned back to the man. "That's my sister, Willow. I'm Rick Forster. We live in that big blue bus."

The man shook Rick's hand heartily. "I'm Dusty Malone. I live up the mountain. In Sandon, an old ghost town."

Rick was impressed.

"I come down once a week," continued Dusty, "to check the beach and deliver ore to the *Moyie*."

"Ore? You mean hunks of rock with silver in them?"

Dusty nodded. "Silver and other minerals. They sell my rock samples in the *Moyie's* visitor centre."

Rick jiggled with excitement. "I collect mineral and rock samples. I can identify twenty-four different minerals."

"I've got a sack full of ore in the yellow truck parked behind your bus," Dusty boasted. "I'll show you when I've finished the beach."

Willow's whistle pierced the air again.

Rick looked back impatiently.

"Come on!" Willow hollered bossily. "It's breakfast time. Mom says."

Irritated, Rick flapped his arm to show he'd heard. "I'll see you up at the truck then?" he said to Dusty.

Dusty nodded absently, concentrating on the next square in the sand.

Willow was eating from a bowl piled high with two types of cereal and slices of banana when Rick hopped on the bus.

"You're going to get it."

"Why? I was only on the beach," Rick said defensively as he grabbed his bowl and filled it. "I met this guy, Dusty," he continued between spoonfuls of cereal. "He's a prospector. He lives in a ghost town and said—"

"Rick Forster, you should know better than taking off without telling us." Their mom appeared, towel-drying her hair.

Willow flashed a told-you-so look at Rick.

"I wasn't, Mom," Rick protested. "I was just outside, at the bottom of the steps. You would have seen me if you'd looked."

"I did look and I didn't see you. Remember the rules—tell us where you're going, or leave your dad and me a note. *Don't* take off on your own. If you can't cope with that, we'll organize a sitter while we're teaching. Okay?"

"Come on, Mom, I told Willow. I banged on her door. Didn't I?"

Willow nodded, her mouth full.

"And you promised, now that Willow's twelve, we could look after ourselves in Kaslo." Rick's voice rose in frustration. "I was within reach. Honest."

Shari Jennings dumped the towel and spiked up her short dark hair. She poured a juice and joined the kids at the table.

"Your dad and I don't like waking up to find that you've vanished. We haven't even had time to check out Kaslo."

"Okay, Okay, I'm sorry. But this guy down there, he's real interesting...He woke me up. I heard his metal detector. He finds neat stuff, and he lives in a ghost town, and he's a pro—pro—prospector looking for silver. An' there's a lost boulder of pure silver nearly as high as a man, and Dusty's parked behind us and promised to show me some chunks of ore, and no one mines for gold around here, it's silver and lead and stuff, and did you know there's an old sternwheeler just up the beach and we can go on her at nine-thirty if it's okay? Can we, can we?"

Rick finally ran out of breath.

Shari and Willow burst out laughing as Rick and Willow's dad appeared from the bedroom.

"Mom and I have to be at the Langham Centre at nine-thirty." Marty Forster pushed aside the juice glasses and placed a map of the town on the table. "Here's where we're parked and here's the Langham." He peered at the map again. "And...here's the sternwheeler you mentioned. Kaslo is tiny, so everything is within a few blocks. Finish breakfast and we'll take a walk and get oriented."

Become a pebble pup

Why not become a pebble pup (a young rockhound), and collect rocks and minerals? Rocks and minerals can be found on beaches or in quarries, natural outcrops, or fields all over Canada. Many provinces publish books showing where special minerals occur. Other samples can be purchased.

All you need to become a pebble pup is a rock pick or hammer, a chisel, and a pair of goggles to protect your eyes against flying chips of rock. Identify your samples with a book on mineral identification from your public library.

A nearby museum may exhibit local discoveries. (If you don't live close to a museum, some big museums show pictures of their finest specimens on the Internet). Some museum stores sell boxed collections of local minerals— or your school may already have one in its teaching kits. If you become a keen pebble pup, consider joining a local rockhound organization or museum club.

www.nmnh.si.edu/minsci/images/gallery/mineral.htm
www.canadianrockhound.com/junior.html
http://rockhoundingar.com/pebblepups.html

"But I promised I'd meet Dusty to look at his ore samples. Can I do that first?"

Marty raised his eyebrows questioningly at his wife and daughter. Neither objected.

"Fine, but finish your breakfast."

CHAPTER THREE

Dusty had not yet returned to the truck, so Willow and Rick fooled around with a hackysack.

Rick kneed it towards Willow. It shot through the open doorway of the small café.

"Oops. You better get it." Willow placed her hands on her hips.

"You get it. You missed it."

"Your aim was off."

"Your hackysack, your problem." Rick turned and ran back to Dusty's truck.

Willow made a rude gesture and entered the café.

Melissa Tomi sat at a table, fingering an old leather diary.

"More coffee, miss?"

Melissa pushed her cup towards the waitress. "Thanks."

The girl looked about Melissa's age, eighteen. Melissa paid tribute to her grandfather. His small legacy meant she didn't have to wait tables this summer. Instead she'd bought a car, waved goodbye to Lethbridge, Alberta, and her disapproving parents, and driven to British Columbia to find out if the story in her grandfather's diary was true.

She nervously fingered the little brown leather book again. Well, here she was. Now what?

She opened the diary at random and looked once more at the tiny crabbed Japanese writing. It was hard to decipher and the pencil had faded in many places. She wished she'd paid more attention when her grandmother had tried to teach her to read and write Japanese.

Melissa flipped through the pages. The Japanese symbol for silver appeared several times. Silver—the stuff her dreams were made of. She laid the diary on the table and sipped her coffee.

A burst of laughter brought Melissa out of her trance. Outside, a couple of kids were playing. Suddenly their hackysack shot through the doorway and slid across the café floor.

"Sorry." With a charming smile, Willow entered the café and looked around.

One of the old men pointed to where the hackysack had slid under Melissa's table.

Willow dropped to all fours and crawled under. As she backed out and stood up, she jiggled the table. Coffee slopped onto a small brown book.

Willow flushed with embarrassment. She grabbed a napkin and started blotting the book. "I'm *really* sorry."

Melissa snatched the book out of Willow's hand. "That's private."

Willow flushed even redder. "I— I —." Mortified, she bolted out of the café.

Upset, Melissa finished wiping the diary. She replaced it carefully in her purse and paid her bill.

>>>>>>>>>>>>> **Writing in Japanese** <<<<<<<<<<<<<

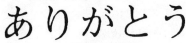

銀　　　ありがとう
Silver　　　　　　**Thank You**

Do you remember learning to write? Once you could remember the 26 letters of our alphabet, each representing a sound, you could learn how to write any word. Japanese children have a much harder task, for their language is written with three different sets of characters.

The Japanese developed their own writing by borrowing characters from Chinese. Two different sets of symbols, called Hiragana and Katakana, represent syllables. Many more borrowed signs (Kanji) are also used for words.

By the time Japanese children leave high school, they need to be familiar with Hiragana, Katakana and around 3000 Kanji. Many students learn our alphabet (Romaji) as well, because it is used to write in Japanese about science and technology, where many of the words come from European languages.

http://members.aol.com/writejapan/index.htm#write
www.sf.airnet.ne.jp/~ts/japanese/index.html

>>>>>>>>>>>>>>>>>>>>>>>>>>>>>>><<<<<<<<<<<<<<<<<<<<<<<<<<<<<<<

25

Dusty Malone dropped the tailgate of his pickup with a loud clang and dragged an old sack to the edge. He opened it and pulled out a palm-sized rock. "Take a look at that."

Still smarting from the hackysack episode, Willow grabbed at it.

"Lay off." Rick pushed Willow aside. "Me first." He snatched the rock and cradled it in his hand.

Dusty slyly handed a larger piece to Willow. She smirked at her brother.

Rick ignored her. He turned his rock from side to side and watched the minerals sparkle in the sunlight.

"My rock's full of gold!" Willow thrust her piece under Rick's nose. "See? It's beautiful."

"Fool's gold," said Dusty flatly.

Rick nodded in agreement.

"Pardon?" Willow stared at Dusty.

"Fool's gold. Deceived a lot of people." Dusty sat on the tailgate and held up another chunk of ore. "See the green-blue colour?"

Both kids peered at the sample.

"It's copper, isn't it?" said Rick eagerly.

Dusty nodded. "So are the pink bits. But the faint yellow, now that's a trace of gold."

"*That's* gold?" exclaimed Willow. "But the big shiny yellow crystals look much more important."

Dusty laughed. "That's why it's called fool's gold. Its real name is iron pyrites. It's worthless."

"So where's the silver?" asked Rick.

Dusty pointed a dirty finger at the few silvery specks on the rock.

"That's not much. You couldn't mine that." Rick sounded disappointed.

Dusty laughed again. "Darned right. These are the tailings…castoffs from the mines. I got them from the discard piles of rock that miners chipped away to reach the main seam. But some of those seams, *they* were rich."

"Like the silver boulder you told Rick about?" asked Willow.

Dusty's eyes suddenly glowed fanatically. "My grandfather found it. A gigantic chunk of rock that had fallen down a cliff. It was lead ore—galena—with silver through and through. And know what?"

Willow and Rick shook their heads.

"Grandfather found it, so the silver boulder should be mine." Dusty scowled and thumped his chest forcefully with his index finger.

Willow took a step backwards and Rick's eyes widened.

No one noticed Melissa Tomi pausing near the truck to listen.

"Grandfather registered it," Dusty maintained fiercely. "Then he and his partner argued over the registration certificate, something about whose or how many names were on it. They were on the *Moyie* over there and there was a scuffle. His partner snatched the certificate, tore it up, and dropped the bits overboard. Then they really hammered each other—a big bust-up on the deck, with half the town cheering them on."

All heads swivelled to look at the sternwheeler basking peacefully in the sunshine.

"Who won?" asked Rick eagerly.

"No one. Grandfather's neck was broken."

Both kids let their breath out in a big whoosh.

"His partner was tried for murder," continued Dusty, "and the whole town was involved in the court case. It was the biggest entertainment for weeks in these parts. That trial was retried every night in the bars—still is when the old-timers have had a skin full. Then, one night while everyone was carousing, the claims office burned down."

"On purpose?" asked Willow.

"Naw, a chimney fire in the house next door. In those days there were always chimney fires. The whole block went up in smoke, and with it the only other record of where the silver boulder was."

Dusty turned and pointed dramatically at the mountains behind him.

"Somewhere out there, it's still waiting for me." His voice rang up and down Front Street. "And I'm gonna *find* it."

Willow shifted nervously. Something about Dusty's fervour made her uncomfortable.

Rick's eyes shone with excitement. "We can help, can't we, Willow? We're here all month with nothing to do. We can help you explore."

A faint gasp behind them made Willow turn.

Now it was Melissa's turn to flush with embarrassment. She walked away quickly.

Puzzled, Willow stared after her. "That girl was listening to us."

"So what," retorted Rick. "Let's start looking for the silver boulder!"

CHAPTER FOUR

Dusty gave a great bray of laughter. "*You?* I've been searching for that boulder for years. How could *you* find it?"

Rick flushed, and Willow leapt to his defence. "You never know. We found an old painting last summer that turned out to be valuable."

Dusty, still chuckling and shaking his head, replaced his rock inside the sack and reknotted the neck.

"You forgot these," said Rick quietly, holding out the ore sample but not meeting Dusty's eyes.

"Keep them. I've got plenty more." Dusty refastened the tailgate, then turned again to Willow and Rick. "Didn't mean to pour cold water on you. Tell you what…"

Rick looked up eagerly.

"I'll see you on the *Moyie* when it opens—got to take the ore anyway. The visitor centre has a big display about mining. There's an old map of all the known mines in this area. I'll show you where I've searched."

"Right on," said Rick. "See you there."

"Idiot," said Willow as they walked back to the bus. "You shouldn't have said anything."

"Do you think we *could* find the silver boulder?" Rick asked her.

"Dunno." Willow held her ore sample up in the sun and watched the fool's gold sparkle. She grinned. "But it'd be fun to try."

Melissa half walked, half ran back to her motel. She unlocked the door with trembling hands and collapsed angrily on the bed.

"I hate this place. Everything seemed straightforward in Lethbridge, but it's different here. I don't fit in." She glanced uneasily down at her cream pants and silk top. "And that hippie. He told those kids about his grandfather and a silver boulder. There can't be *two* silver boulders."

She opened her purse, pulled out the diary, and riffled through until she found the page she wanted.

Squinting at the tiny pencil marks, she once more laboriously translated. "A giant of a rock...shining silver..." She flipped to another page. "Reflected in the creek..." She stopped and shook her head when she couldn't understand the next bit.

Melissa closed the diary, rolled over onto her back, and thought about her grandfather's story. "That hippie's grandfather...He must be the person who tried to steal the silver boulder off *my* grandfather."

She turned and thumped the pillow. "I've got to find it before anyone else. I've got to. I've got to."

The Forster-Jennings family walked around Kaslo and ended up opposite the historic Langham Cultural Centre. They stopped to admire its elegant exterior.

Willow nudged Rick. "There's that girl again," she whispered.

Melissa appeared around the corner of the Langham. She read a plaque fixed to the wall, then she blew her nose hard and disappeared inside.

"She read something that upset her," observed Rick. "Weird." He ran across the road to read the plaque himself. "Hey, look at this. The Langham wasn't just a rooming house, it was a…" He ran his finger over the plaque and read out loud, "A detention centre for Japanese…Is that like a prison?" He stopped and looked up at the building again. "Why?"

Marty sighed. "It happened a long time ago…during the last world war. Canada was fighting against Japan as well as Germany. There were a lot of Japanese Canadians living on the B.C. coast. The Canadian government was scared they would help Japan instead of Canada. So it rounded them up and shipped them to other places to live, far away from the coast. Kaslo was one of the places they came to."

"It says there's an exhibit on the top floor. Let's look," said Willow.

"Enemy aliens" at home

How would you feel if your neighbours suddenly said you were an enemy and sent you away? That's what happened to Canadian citizens of Japanese heritage during World War II.

Canada had over 23 000 residents of Japanese origin. Most had come from Japan and become Canadian citizens. Many had been born in Canada, and some had fought for Canada in World War I.

In December 1941, the Japanese made a surprise attack on Pearl Harbor in Hawaii, followed by attacks on Hong Kong, which was protected by Canadian troops. Suddenly Canada was at war with Japan. Japanese schools and most Japanese-language newspapers were closed. The Canadian government shipped Japanese Canadian residents away from the coast, with only one suitcase each. The property they left behind was taken away and eventually sold.

The government claimed it was protecting Canada from saboteurs and spies, but its actions were partly prompted by racism. Not one Japanese Canadian was prosecuted for spying. After the war, many Japanese Canadians were forced to "return" to Japan—a country some of them had never seen. Others were dispersed around the country. The Canadian government finally apologized for its wartime treatment of Japanese Canadians in 1998.

www.bcarchives.gov.bc.ca/exhibits/timemach/galler05/frames /index.htm

www.queensu.ca/idis/japan/index.htm

"You go. We'll see it later. It's time for our meeting. The Arts Festival office is on the second floor. Speak to the secretary, Mrs. Dreger, if you need us." Marty suddenly became brisk and businesslike. "Have you both got cash?"

"Yup." Rick jingled his pockets and Willow patted her fanny pack.

"You know where we are if there's a problem. Meet us here at noon for lunch."

"Have fun," said Shari, and both parents left.

Rick and Willow wandered around the exhibit. They looked at old photos and gazed uncomfortably at a room set up to show the sad realities of Japanese internment.

"Look at that." Rick tried to lighten things up. "Boy, do they look miserable." Laughing, he pointed to a yellowed photo of a young Japanese couple and a tiny baby.

As if by magic, a white-faced Melissa Tomi materialized before him. "You'd look miserable if you'd been forced from your house, only allowed to take a small suitcase of belongings, then imprisoned for years when you had done nothing wrong!"

Rick and Willow stared open-mouthed at her.

Melissa looked as though she was going to say something else, but she turned and ran into the washroom.

"What's with her?" asked Rick, confused.

Willow shrugged. "Maybe she was offended because you were laughing?"

35

The three-storey Langham building was built in 1892 and housed banks and businesses on the ground floor, while people lived above. By the 1930s, it was empty except for a lumber store.

In 1942, when Kaslo became home to 1100 Japanese Canadians, more than seventy people were moved into the old place, one family per room. During their first winter there, the town had two metres of snow and the residents had to patch the leaky walls with newspaper.

Many of the men were forced to work in lumber mills or on road construction. Everyone carried an "Enemy Alien Identification Card," and phone calls in the Japanese language were forbidden. The children were not allowed to attend the local school, so in spring, classes were set up in the parks and on the beaches.

In 1974, the Langham Cultural Society was formed to buy and preserve the old building and turn it into an arts centre. On the third floor, a restoration of 1941 conditions shows how Japanese residents had to live. The society now sponsors the Kaslo-on-the-Lake Summer School of the Arts.

www.kin.bc.ca/langham/langhom.htm

"I wasn't laughing at her, I wasn't really laughing at anyone—I was just trying to make a joke."

Willow shrugged again. "She's Japanese. This exhibit probably upset her." She squeezed Rick's shoulder. "Don't worry about it. We'll stay out of her way."

"Okay." Rick looked around the room one last time. "Let's get out of here and go visit the sternwheeler. Race you!"

CHAPTER FIVE

WWWHOOOOOOOoooooooooo.

The ship's whistle rang through the town. There was no mistaking it. Willow and Rick looked up to see someone grinning down at them from the pilothouse at the very top of the sternwheeler.

"It's Dusty," said Rick, waving. "Come on." He led the way into the interpretive centre and the entrance to the S.S. *Moyie*.

There was an exhibit on mining in the interpretive centre, displays of rocks and minerals, and photos of the old miners. Rick was fascinated by the rock specimens and showed Willow which samples he already had in his collection.

"There's about six minerals here I don't have. I wonder if Dusty found them," he said enviously. "Do you think he'd show us where we could collect some?"

Willow shrugged. "Who knows? But it's a neat idea. We've got the geological picks from our geology course. I've never used mine."

Rick swung an imaginary pick and made chinking sounds with his tongue. "I have. Remember? I collected some stuff on the beach in Vancouver."

They made their way to the entrance, paid their fee, and ran along the walkway to the newly built landing stage for the *Moyie*.

"You can't tell the *Moyie's* beached from this side," said Rick. "With the lake spread out behind, she looks as though she's waiting for her next load of passengers and cargo."

Willow was immediately caught up in the sense of history. "Yeah, look at that old car." She pointed to a display by the ship's cargo doors. "And see the old-fashioned cart with all the luggage piled on it? It's like we're the passengers. Once we're on board, she'll blow the whistle and head off up the lake."

"You ain't seen nothing yet." Dusty hung over the upper deck railing. "Go inside and look at the chickens."

The kids ran up the gangway onto the cargo deck and entered the maze of equipment and cargo in the hold. They dodged around the stokehole and wound around the levers and steam pipes in the engine room. Rick's hand snaked out to pull one of the levers.

"Don't touch a thing," bellowed Dusty bossily, coming up behind him.

Rick leapt backwards guiltily.

They wandered through the cargo area, stacked high with tubs of lard, crates of apples, and sacks of flour, and peered into the boilers. They looked into the ship's galley, skirted around piles of lumber, another car, and, sure enough, an antique truck full of crates of chickens.

"You can even hear them clucking," chuckled Willow. She looked around in amazement. "It's all so real."

"You're right, me girl. This is exactly how the *Moyie* looked in her prime. She hauled goods like this up and down Kootenay Lake."

Willow and Rick turned to see who was talking.

A white-bearded old man dressed in a captain's uniform solemnly saluted them. "Captain Olund at your service. I'm the curator of the *Moyie*. I'd be happy to answer your questions."

"Are you really a captain, or just dressed up as one?" asked Rick.

"I was the last captain of the *Moyie*," answered the old man proudly.

"Brought her down to Kaslo on her final run in 1957." He proudly brushed an invisible speck of lint off his jacket. "Lots of people want to wear this uniform. To act the part. One man even offered me sixty dollars. But I'm the only one who's entitled to wear it. I'm the last of 'em. The last living sternwheeler captain."

His eyes grew misty. Then he patted the side of the ship affectionately and laughed. "But the *Moyie*'s in better shape than me. She's been restored and rebuilt. She's almost as good now as the day she came off the slip."

"Could she sail again?" Rick looked around curiously.

"Well, she's beached in a cradle, but everything is in working order, even the paddle. It's all been rebuilt." The captain stopped and peered at them. "You want to see her?"

"You bet," said Willow.

"Yeah, everything," agreed Rick.

"Then let's start at the top and work down. First, I'll show you my eyrie, the pilothouse."

Rick galloped up the stairs after the captain. Willow followed more slowly. As they entered the Smoking Saloon, Rick paused. "Uh-uh," he muttered, then bent his head down and followed the captain up the next set of stairs to the top of the ship.

Willow looked around to see what had bothered her younger brother. Wicker chairs and small tables were scattered around the cabin, but in the middle was a display case containing small objects. Bending over it intently was the Japanese girl. Something odd, almost secretive, in the girl's manner intrigued Willow. She hung back in the shadow of the stairway and watched.

The girl glanced swiftly around the cabin, then she produced the small brown leather diary from her shoulder purse. She opened it to the middle and studied a page. Holding it over the display case, she looked from the book to the display as though trying to match them up.

A young couple, laughing and talking, came in the far doorway. In one movement, the girl closed the book and moved away from the display to gaze out the saloon's rear

The S.S. *Moyie* — "Sweetheart of the Lake" <<<

For nearly sixty years, the steamship *Moyie* sailed up and down Kootenay Lake, travelling more than 3 million kilometres. Linking the lakeside communities together, she became known as the "sweetheart of the lake." She was the last passenger-carrying sternwheeler to operate in western North America, and she is the oldest surviving ship of her kind in the world.

In 1898, the *Moyie* was shipped in pieces from Toronto to Nelson, where she was built and named after a nearby mining community. She was 49 metres long and 10 metres wide. Her flat bottom allowed her to float in only a metre of water.

The *Moyie* and other sternwheelers plied Kootenay Lake. They carried passengers and freight to many lakeside communities. Sometimes two steamers ran a race, or an excursion was arranged. It was a big event when the steamer came to town, and everyone raced to the dock to meet her.

As roads were built, steamboat traffic decreased, and the *Moyie* was retired in 1957. She began her second career, as Kaslo's museum. In 1978, she was declared a National Historic Site, and detailed restoration began. Now the *Moyie* welcomes thousands of visitors every year.

www.kin.bc.ca/Archives/Moyie/MoyieHome1.html
www.crowsnest.bc.ca/ssmoyie.html
http://rbcm1.rbcm.gov.bc.ca/notes/sternwhe.html

windows. Willow seized the chance to slip through and follow the others to the pilothouse.

Perched on the highest point of the upper deck of the S.S. *Moyie,* the pilothouse was all windows, giving a bird's-eye view of the lake and Kaslo. Dusty and the captain were already squished to one side of the ship's gigantic wheel. Rick stood on the other side. He motioned Willow to join him.

"Did you see her?" he whispered.

"Shhhh. Tell you later," replied Willow.

Captain Olund proudly demonstrated how he'd stood at the wheel to steer, and pointed to a large wooden lever overhead.

"Know what that is?"

Willow eyed it. "The brake?"

Dusty roared with laughter and slapped his knee. "That's a good one, a ship's brake."

Willow glared at him, wishing she'd kept her mouth shut.

Captain Olund smiled gently and looked questioningly at Rick.

Rick shrugged.

The captain looked back at Willow. "Want to try?"

Willow raised her arm and pulled the lever. An ear-piercing whistle rang out. She instantly let go and both kids clapped their hands over their ears.

"It sure made people skedaddle," Captain Olund said. "Had to. Once the *Moyie* was under steam, I couldn't stop her quickly."

"Should have used the brake," interjected Dusty, and cracked out laughing again.

Willow eyed him with dislike.

"It also warned folks I was coming. So they could gather on the beach to meet me."

"The beach?" questioned Willow. "Didn't you use a dock?"

"The miners' camps were all over the place, and many were temporary. There were no docks. The *Moyie* was built with a shallow draft—a flat bottom—so I could bring her into a beach. That way I could drop off supplies almost anywhere up the lake."

Captain Olund pointed out places of interest in the town below and told stories from Kaslo's past.

Dusty was really getting on Willow's nerves. Every time the captain told a story, Dusty had a better one. Every time the captain pointed out a historic site, Dusty pointed out another one. The captain's stories were funny and interesting, but Dusty's comments always had a nasty side.

"Ah, those were good days," sighed the captain. "There was always something funny happening. One day, the stoker came to me. 'Think you better go to the galley,' he said. 'Cook's scrubbing the meat.' 'Scrubbing the meat?' I asked. 'Yup, with the scrubbing brush.' Well, down I went, and sure enough the cook was going at a side of beef with the big wire brush we used on the decks. 'Why in tarnation are you doing that?' I asked. 'Meat's green,' he answered and started scrubbing again."

"Green meat. Yuk." Willow wrinkled her nose.

Captain Olund guffawed. "I guess it had been in the ice box a mite too long. I threw the whole lot overboard." He shook his head and chuckled again. "Scrubbing the meat, eh…scrubbing the meat!"

"What do you expect from a Chinese cook?" said Dusty dismissively.

Willow and the captain exchanged dismayed looks.

The captain changed the subject, telling them about some of the old-timers he'd worked with.

Good. Now Dusty will have to shut up 'cause he's not that old, thought Willow with satisfaction.

"Were you captain when Dusty's grandfather was murdered?" interrupted Rick innocently.

The captain paused, then shot a disapproving look at Dusty. "You filling their heads with rubbish?" He turned sternly to the children. "Was he?"

"He—he told us about his grandfather—and—and the lost silver boulder," Rick stammered.

"Hmph. Take it with a pinch of salt. There's two sides to a story." The captain shook his finger in Dusty's face. "Don't try to rewrite history, Dusty Malone. The whole town knows your grandfather was a scoundrel who tried to double-cross poor old Boulder Bob. That's why his ghost won't rest in peace."

The captain glared at Dusty, stomped out of the pilot-house and down the stairs.

"Take no notice. He's a mad old coot." An embarrassed Dusty tried to laugh off the captain's remarks. "Look—I've gotta go. I'll see you around town, eh?" Dusty bolted like a rabbit down the narrow stairs.

"Did Dusty lie to us?" asked Rick.

Willow shrugged. "What about the ghost stuff? Weird, eh?"

"If we can find the captain again, maybe he'll tell us. He wasn't mad at us, was he? Just Dusty."

"Dusty gives me the creeps," said Willow. "I don't want to hang around with him any more. He's strange."

"I know," agreed Rick. "He seemed okay at first, but he gets pretty worked up about the boulder."

"And weird things keep happening. You saw the Japanese girl in the Smoking Saloon?"

"Yup. That's why I rushed through. I didn't want her to see me."

"Well, I spied on her. She was looking at something in the display case and checking it against a little book. But she didn't want anyone to see her doing it."

"Weirder and weirder."

The two kids climbed down from the pilothouse and entered the sumptuous Ladies' Saloon, with its red plush upholstery and elegant gold moulding around the ceiling. It was empty. They wandered around, leaning into the passenger cabins that opened off each side, to see the museum displays.

"Rick, over here. Listen." Willow pointed and Rick peeked into a cabin displaying models of a mother and baby curled up in a bunk together. The mother was singing nursery rhymes to the child.

47

"Cute." Rick grinned. "Hey, when we were downstairs, did you hear all the cooking noises from the galley? You could hear fat sizzling and dishes and pots clanging."

"Yeah, but I didn't hear anyone scrubbing meat," Willow answered. They both cracked up.

"It's so cool," said Rick. "The sounds really make everything seem real."

"You have to be careful with sounds on this ship." The captain's voice startled them. "There's some you don't bargain on."

The kids looked warily at the captain.

He beckoned them over to a table and chairs. "I'll rest my pins."

He sat down with a bump. "And tell you about the silver boulder and the ghost."

"Whose ghost?" asked Willow. "Boulder Bob's?"

The captain chuckled wheezily. "Naw, Boulder Bob's alive and kicking in Sandon."

His chuckle turned into a cough and he hacked away for a few minutes, then blew his nose and wiped his eyes. "Now about that boulder..." He dropped his voice, and the kids drew their chairs closer.

"No one really knows the rights and wrongs of who found it first. There was someone else involved, but old Bob clammed up and wouldn't say. But we all knew Boulder Bob and Meddlesome Malone."

"Malone?" questioned Rick. "As in Dusty's grandfather?"

"That's right, and 'meddlesome,' as in having a finger in every scheme in this town, particularly the crooked ones. Now listen up."

The kids leaned in towards the captain.

"Meddlesome put a quick one over on Boulder. Boulder Bob couldn't read or write, see. He needed someone to fill in a claim form for him, and of course Meddlesome Malone offered to help out."

"But why let him if everyone knew he was a crook?" asked Willow.

"Ah, Boulder lived in Sandon, so didn't know him that well. Besides, Boulder Bob always believed the best of everyone. But when he found out he'd been double-crossed, he got wild. The fight was out there on the deck. We all saw it. They were throwing punches right and left. Then Bob got lucky, or unlucky, I guess. He hit Malone on the jaw and Malone staggered back, through the gap to the companionway. Down the stairs he went. And that was the end of him—Malone broke his neck."

There was a long silence. Then the captain looked uneasily over his shoulder, leaned across the table, and continued in a whisper. "But Meddlesome Malone, he knew what he'd done was wrong. I reckon that's why... sometimes...I hear his ghost falling down those stairs... again...and again...and again."

As his voice faded away, there was a soft sound, then a faint gasp, and the sound of a body falling down the stairs.

CHAPTER SIX

They all froze for an instant before pushing back their chairs and racing to the head of the companionway. Willow and Rick arrived first and stared down.

Melissa Tomi sat on the deck below, rubbing her knee and shin. She looked up with watery eyes. "I'm all right, I think...I just banged my leg. It was my own fault. I... I..." She closed her eyes and a few tears oozed through her lashes.

"Oh there, there." Captain Olund pushed between Willow and Rick and clambered down the companionway. He pulled a large white handkerchief out of his pocket and thrust it into Melissa's hands. He glanced up at the kids. "One of you run to the interpretive centre. Ask them to call the doctor."

"No," Melissa blurted out. "No, I'm okay. I don't need it."

Willow and Rick looked uncertainly from her to the captain. He shrugged.

"No, please." Melissa wiped her eyes with the handkerchief and pulled herself to her feet. "I'm fine. Honestly."

She brushed some dirt off her jeans and leaned against the wall. "It was just a shock. I'll be fine in a few minutes."

The captain offered his arm and helped her to a bench.

Willow nudged Rick. "Come on," she whispered. "Let's go down."

"What for?" Rick muttered stubbornly.

Willow nudged him again. "Come on. Maybe we'll find out why she's been acting so strange."

Rick shook his head violently. "No way. Let's get out of here and explore Kaslo. She's bad news. I'm not hanging around *her*."

"Yeah, you're right."

They sneaked away, leaving the captain to cope.

Melissa blew her nose. "This is so embarrassing."

Captain Olund clumsily patted her arm.

"I forgot the stairs were behind me," she continued.

"You were listening to us?" asked the captain.

Melissa rubbed her leg and looked uncomfortable. "I heard you all talking about the silver boulder and… well…I'm looking for it, too." Tears glistened in her eyes. "I'm sorry." She blew her nose firmly. "I didn't mean to listen…well, I did…but I need some help. I don't know who to go to."

A gust of cold wind swept along the deck and Melissa shivered.

"Well, well, well." The captain scratched his beard.

"I can't say as I understand all this. But maybe I can help if I hear a straight story."

Another gust of wind lifted the captain's cap. He clamped it back on and eyed the sky. "The weather's changing. We won't see the sun for a while."

He eyed Melissa's leg. "If you could climb the stairs again, we could sit in the saloon and sort this out in comfort."

Melissa sniffed and smiled. "My leg really is okay. I just bruised it. Nothing is twisted or broken." She stood up. "See?" She walked stiffly to the stairs and slowly climbed up.

Once again the captain sat at the table, but this time Melissa sat with him, her leg resting on another chair.

"I'm Captain Olund." The captain gestured towards her. "And you are?"

Melissa shifted nervously. "Melissa Tomi. I'm from Lethbridge, but my grandfather was detained in Kaslo during the war."

"Stayed at the Langham, did he?" asked the captain with interest.

"Yes. Before that, he and Grandma were in Sandon. They lived there for several years. My father was born there."

"Tomi, Tomi. It rings a bell. I might have met your grandfather," the captain mused.

Melissa blew her nose again. "Grandma died years ago, but Grandfather lived until April. He was ninety-three," she added proudly. "He only told a few stories about Sandon and Kaslo. But there was this one story he told many times. My family kind of joked about it. Grandfather supposedly found a boulder of silver but wasn't able to claim it because he was an 'enemy alien.' When his partner tried to help, they were double-crossed. None of us took the story seriously. Then when Grandfather died, he left me this."

>>>>>>>>> **If your dad was a miner** <<<<<<<<

In the old days, if your dad was a miner you would see him walk to the mine every morning. Perhaps you went partway with him on your way to school. He'd keep his tools— hammers and drills and shovels—at the mine, and over supper he'd talk about digging shafts and levels, or finding a rich vein. Perhaps he had a mule or horse to haul out the ore, and you'd get to ride on it.

At weekends and holidays you'd help around the house, then watch the ore being loaded in the railcars, and hope to see the steam locomotive that would haul them down to the concentrator in Kaslo.

Sometimes you might ride the buckets hanging on cables that carried supplies up the hills, or be taken into the cold, wet, scary mine. You'd hope your dad would be careful, and not have an accident.

>>>>>>>>>>>>>>>>>>>>>>>>>>>>>>>>>>>>>>><<<<<<<<<<<<<<<<<<<<<<<<<<<<<<<<<<<<<<<<

Melissa reached in her purse and brought out the small leather book, laying it on the table.

"It's the journal he kept when they lived in Sandon. It's in Japanese but I can read some of it." She flicked open the pages and pointed. "Here, and here, and here. This is the character for silver. He really did find something important. There's even a map." She opened the diary to the middle and showed him. "But half is missing. It's been torn out. I think the missing part would have showed the lake and Kaslo, some major landmark that would orient the map. Without it, it's hard to figure out where the boulder was." She half laughed. "I even tried to match up this map with the old one in your display case." She pointed. "But it was hopeless."

Melissa closed the diary and sighed. "I wanted to do something special with Grandfather's legacy, so I bought a used car with his money. Then I came to Kaslo to see if the silver boulder story was true." She looked apologetically at the captain. "When you started telling the story to those kids, I couldn't help but listen."

Captain Olund shifted in his seat and waggled his eyebrows. "Well, that's quite a story. Tomi…Tomi? Your story is beginning to make sense."

He stood up creakily. "All of Kaslo knew there was another person involved in the claim with Boulder Bob, but Bob's mouth was shut tighter than a steel trap. It never even came out in court. If it was your grandfather, that would make sense. We weren't supposed to fraternize with enemy aliens, though unofficially several of us made friends."

Captain Olund replaced his chair carefully under the table and motioned to Melissa. "Come through to the mining exhibit. I'll give you a photocopy of the map of this area, the same as the one in the display case. You can check it against the half map you have there. But I think you should drive up to Sandon, young lady. Go find Boulder Bob. Tell him Captain Olund sent you."

CHAPTER SEVEN

Dusty Malone was mad. He angrily shifted the gears in his pickup and they groaned in protest. "I hate that captain…interfering old buzzard." Dusty slammed his foot to the floor, and the old pickup bucketed around the corner, rattled down one hill, and heaved its way protesting up the next.

"I shouldn't have bothered with that kid. Thinks he could find the silver boulder, huh." Dusty impatiently ground the gearbox again. "Stupid kid."

He drove for a while, steadily climbing the long valley into the mountains behind Kaslo, thoughts buzzing around his head. "Gotta find it though. Gotta lean on Boulder Bob again. He knows something for sure. Maybe…if I'm nice to him. He's getting on. If I help him out a bit…maybe…he'll forget about my grandfather and talk. Must be lonely on his own at the far end of Sandon. Yup, tomorrow I'll offer to chop some wood for the old guy. See if I can get him spilling the beans."

Dusty relaxed and started whistling tunelessly.

He turned the pickup onto the rough gravel road that led to Sandon.

"Goodness, is it lunchtime already?" Shari Jennings gave her kids an absent-minded smile. "Enjoyed your morning?"

Rick and Willow grinned slyly at each other.

Shari leaned across the small office and nudged her husband in the back. "Marty—it's lunchtime. Come on. Our guest will be waiting."

"Guest? Who else is coming?" asked Willow.

"I'm constantly amazed at what a small world we live in." Marty logged off the computer and swivelled around on his chair to grin at his kids. "I met an Alberta connection earlier this morning—I worked with her father last year. She's joining us. Okay?"

"Yeah, sure." The kids were always having lunch with business contacts of one parent or another.

The restaurant was a few blocks away. As they walked together, Willow and Rick described the *Moyie*.

"You've gotta see it," Willow enthused. "It would make an awesome subject for a movie."

"We'll check it out," Marty assured her. He held open the gate to the garden of an old house.

"This is a restaurant? Cool."

"Can we sit in the garden?" asked Rick.

Their parents looked up at the sky. The wind had freshened and clumps of grey clouds scudded across.

"It looks as though it might rain," said Shari doubtfully.

"Besides, I think our guest is waiting inside." Marty opened the front door and waved everyone in.

Rick barrelled forward, then suddenly stopped.

Willow cannoned into him.

Wordlessly he pointed.

Waiting at a table in the bow window was the Japanese girl.

"Ah, Melissa." Marty strode to the table and shook the girl's hand. "Glad you could join us. I'd like you to meet my children." He smiled across at them. "Rick and Willow, this is Melissa Tomi. I met her father and aunt when I filmed the Japanese tea ceremony in Lethbridge last year."

Stunned, Rick and Willow touched hands briefly with Melissa and silently slid into their chairs.

Melissa looked equally shaken.

The silence was deafening.

Shari looked from one to the other. "Is something wrong? Have you three already met?"

Willow looked down at her plate. "Kind of," she muttered.

Rick was more forthright. "She yelled at me in the Japanese exhibit, an—an—she's been following us around eavesdropping ever since."

Melissa burst into tears.

Horrified, Shari and Marty thrust napkins at Melissa, waved away the waiter, and glared at Rick and Willow, who shrugged and said nothing.

"I didn't mean…I wasn't…" Melissa took a napkin and mopped her face.

Shari patted her shoulder gently. "Take a deep breath and let's start again. I'm sure we can sort all this out."

Rick and Willow looked unconvinced.

Melissa took several breaths and wiped her eyes. "This has been an *awful* day." She looked at Willow and Rick. "I do owe you both an apology. And an explanation. I didn't mean to be rude, or yell at you, or even eavesdrop. It just happened that way."

She picked up her purse and pulled out the diary and an old sepia snapshot of a young Japanese couple holding a baby. She pushed the photo over the table toward Rick. "These are my grandparents, with my dad when he was a baby."

Rick groaned. "Oh no. That photo in the exhibit. Is it the same one?"

"Yes," Melissa whispered.

"It was *your* grandparents," Rick spluttered. "I'm–I'm sorry. I wasn't really laughing *at* them, you know. I—I—I was just—that exhibit. It made me feel bad. I was just trying to lighten things up."

"It's okay. I was upset by the exhibit and took it out on you." Melissa ran her fingers through her hair and tried to gather her thoughts.

She turned to Shari and Marty. "It happened just before I met you. I had no idea you were their parents."

She met Rick's eyes again. "It was hard visiting the

Langham. My grandparents were interned there during the war. They didn't really talk about their early life. I hadn't realized what awful conditions they lived in, until I saw the exhibit. It was a shock seeing their photo. It was just up there on its own. Like no one even knew their names." She looked apologetically at both Rick and Willow. "When you laughed, I kinda lost it."

"But why were you eavesdropping on the *Moyie*?" asked Willow suspiciously. "We weren't talking about your grandparents then."

Melissa laughed ruefully. "Actually, you were. The reason I came to Kaslo is in here." She pointed to the diary. "Grandfather wrote it while he was living up in Sandon. It's about him finding a silver boulder and he and his partner being cheated out of it."

"You're joking—it must be about Boulder Bob!" exclaimed Rick.

"And Meddlesome Malone," added Willow, her eyes dancing.

Forgetting all their suspicions, Rick, Willow, and Melissa leaned across the table and pieced together the story.

"There's avocado on my hamburger," said Rick in disgust when they finally got their orders. "No one puts avocado on hamburgers." He opened the bun and furiously scraped at it.

Shari leaned over, lifted the offending item with her knife and smeared it on her veggie burger. "Yummy."

Rick made gagging sounds. His mother glared.

Willow and Melissa smothered grins.

The conversation returned to the mystery of the silver boulder.

"Captain Olund suggested I go to Sandon to meet Boulder Bob," said Melissa. She hesitated. "I don't suppose you would like to come with me?" she asked Rick and Willow.

Brother and sister nudged each other under the table.

"You bet!" they exclaimed.

Shari looked worried. "You don't have to put up with them," she assured Melissa.

"No. Actually it's lonely travelling on my own. I'd like to have them along. In fact, they would be helpful. They seem to chat so easily with older people. A lot easier than I can. As long as it's all right with you?" Melissa finished.

Shari laughed, "They can certainly chat. What do you think, Marty?"

Marty stretched back in his chair. "If Melissa promises to drive carefully, I guess there's no problem. I think Sandon is only half an hour away. When were you thinking of going?"

"This afternoon," Melissa replied.

Shari shook her head decisively. "Sorry, kids. We've got permission to move the bus to the park at the edge of town. We can't leave it parked on Front Street for a month. Then you've got to get on with your schoolwork. You haven't done any yet. You know the deal. Three hours every day."

Rick and Willow's disappointment hung almost visibly in the air.

"Okay. How about tomorrow then," said Melissa.

Rick opened his mouth to protest, but Willow suddenly kicked his ankle. He gasped and rubbed it.

"That's really nice of you, Melissa." Shari smiled at her. "Do you mind waiting to meet Boulder Bob?"

Melissa shook her head. "Actually, it makes more sense. A chance to rest my bruised leg would be great. And I didn't sleep well last night, wondering how I'd find out about the silver boulder." She laughed. "I never dreamt people would be talking about it everywhere I went."

"Can I log onto the Internet while I'm doing my school-work?" asked Willow. She shot a funny glance at Rick.

Rick looked baffled.

"Sure," said Marty. "We made arrangements for you and Rick to use a desk in our office. This afternoon would be good. Your mom and I are taking a walk around Kaslo to check out story ideas and film locations." He looked at his watch. "Come on. Got to get going and move the bus."

He turned to Melissa. "You're sure tomorrow is okay? We didn't ask how long you are going to be in town."

"It's fine." Melissa grinned. "I plan on being around for a while. In fact, until I find it," she finished.

They grinned back.

"Mom, if we do lots of work this afternoon, then some more first thing tomorrow, can we leave mid-morning?" asked Rick.

"I don't see why not," Shari agreed. "As long as your quota for the day is done."

"Excellent," Rick and Willow chorused.

"How about I come by around eleven?" Melissa suggested. "The park is near my motel and I sure can't miss your 'Orca Enterprises' bus."

Everyone chuckled.

Melissa stood up. "Thanks for lunch, Mr. Forster. I'll see you all tomorrow."

"What's up? Why did you kick me?" hissed Rick, hanging back with Willow as they all walked towards the bus.

"Didn't want you arguing about us staying in Kaslo this afternoon," Willow hissed back.

"You didn't?" Rick was still confused.

"I suddenly realized we needed to get on the Net before doing anything else."

"Why, what's the hurry?"

"Think about it, dummy. There are two conflicting stories. Dusty's telling one, Melissa and the captain are telling another. Then there's this Boulder Bob person she's going to see. He could be a murderer. If we're going to look for the silver boulder, we've got to check out a couple of things."

"Oh, I get it," said Rick. "First we check out the stories. Make sure Melissa's grandfather *was* the real owner of the boulder. Then we know we're helping the right side."

"Right."

Rick frowned. "So what's the second thing?"

"We need to find out how to stake a claim."

Rick's face cleared. "Gotcha." He punched Willow's arm. "You're *good*."

Willow smiled smugly.

While Rick did some schoolwork, Willow worked for an hour online with the B.C. Archives. The printer steadily churned out news reports.

She gathered them up and scanned some stories. "It's all here. Reports of Boulder Bob's trial and everything. His real name is Robert McKenzie. Here, take a look."

Rick carefully read several pages.

"So? What do you think? Same thing as me?" prompted Willow.

"That Dusty's a liar?"

"Yep."

"But there's nothing here about Boulder Bob having a partner other than Meddlesome. Nothing about Melissa's grandfather. In fact, nothing about a silver boulder."

"I know. But remember what Captain Olund said. They couldn't show they were friendly with enemy aliens? Look, it's true. There's lots about the Japanese. Some of it pretty scary. Lots of people hated them." Willow stretched and yawned. "I'm going cross-eyed. See what you can find out about the other stuff."

"Move over." Rick shoved Willow off the chair and hunkered down over the keyboard, rapidly typing in key words. Willow tackled her schoolwork, occasionally leaning over to make suggestions.

Finally the printer clattered and Rick gathered up the pages. "Great session." He pulled out a sheet and passed it to Willow. "See? 'How to stake a claim.' Melissa has to find a mining office."

"That's easy," laughed Willow. "We passed one twice today. Didn't you notice?"

Rick shook his head.

"It's just around the corner. We should phone Melissa at the motel. She could stop in before picking us up tomorrow."

Rick retrieved some pages that had slipped to the floor. "I found loads of information on silver, and more about the Japanese internment. I can't believe we didn't know about this. Some really famous people were in the internment camps." He pointed to a name. "See, David Suzuki. He's the guy on TV."

Willow grunted absentmindedly. She was busy checking the phone book.

"There were writers too," Rick continued. "Look." He thrust a page under Willow's nose. "Imagine writing beautiful haiku poetry in prison camps. How could they do that?" Rick's voice trailed off, then rose again. "Look at this one!" He stabbed at the paper. "It was written by someone called Tomi."

At last Rick had Willow's attention. She snatched the paper out of his hand and read it intently.

Moonlight, gift from sky.
Cedar-wrapped rock, gift from earth.
Each reflecting each.

—Tomi

"See—Tomi," Rick said. "Do you think it's Melissa's grandfather?"

Willow grinned. "Last summer you said I was nuts when I thought the sketch we found was a Group of Seven. Now it's my turn. You're nuts! I bet there were loads of people called Tomi."

Rick spun her around on the office chair. "Come on, Willow. You've gotta admit it's an amazing coincidence."

Willow read the poem again. "I wonder what it means? …'cedar-wrapped rock'…Hmmm…Okay. Keep it in case it's a clue. We'll do some more detective work. Let's get Melissa to see if there's anything like it in her grandfather's journal!"

The ancient pond
A frog leaps in
The sound of water

This tiny poem, translated from Japanese, is a well-known example of an old Japanese form of poetry called haiku. Haiku are carefully crafted miniature poems, usually containing a vivid image and an interesting idea. Although they seem simple, they are hard to write well.

Some Western writers have learned to write haiku, and now students like to try them, too. In Canadian schools, students usually follow the Japanese rule, writing haiku in three lines. The first line contains five syllables, the second seven syllables, and the third five again. (Haiku translated from Japanese don't always follow these rules strictly.)

http://cc.matsuyama-u.ac.jp/~shiki/intro.html
www.toyomasu.com/haiku
www.tecnet.or.jp/~haiku/gardEC2.htm

>>>>>>>>>>>>>>>>>>>>>>>>>>>>>>>>>>>><<<<<<<<<<<<<<<<<<<<<<<<<<<<<<

CHAPTER EIGHT

Just before eleven the next morning, Melissa drove up and parked beside the bus.

Rick rushed out to meet her. "*This* is your car?" he said admiringly.

Melissa patted the wheel. "It's secondhand," she replied apologetically.

"It's a 4x4, an SUV. Cool." Rick's eyes gleamed.

"What's an SUV?" Willow questioned, coming up behind.

Rick looked pityingly at her. "Sport Utility Vehicle, idiot." He turned back to Melissa. "It will go up forestry roads and—and do off-roading. You can go anywhere in this. It will be perfect for searching for the silver boulder."

Melissa grinned and her usually serious face lit up. "That's why I got it," she said. "My parents had a fit." She suddenly giggled, seeming closer in age to Willow and Rick. The slight stiffness between the three of them vanished.

"Okay," said Rick, brandishing his geological pick, "let's load up and go."

"Oh you'll never get to heaven."

"Oh you'll never get to heaven."

"In a four-wheel drive."

"In a four-wheel drive," everyone chorused, then hesitated…

"You'll bounce so high, you won't survive," suggested Rick.

"For a four-wheel drive will give you hives," sang Willow. The song dissolved into laughter.

"Don't distract me," said Melissa in mock anger. "This mountain road is narrow and twisting. It needs all my attention. Check the map, Willow. How far to Sandon?"

"Should be soon. Watch for a gravel road going off to the left."

Rick hummed quietly while Melissa drove.

"Melissa?" Willow suddenly asked. "Did you read all of your grandfather's diary?"

"What I could. My Japanese is pretty rusty. Why?"

"Well, when we were on the Net yesterday, Rick found a bunch of haiku poems written by people in the camps. There was one by someone called Tomi. We wondered if your grandfather wrote any."

"I'm not sure," said Melissa thoughtfully. "I don't know if my Japanese is good enough to pick them up from his journal. Remind me to look when we get back."

"There's the sign for Sandon," sang out Rick.

Melissa flicked on the indicator, and the 4x4 bounced onto the potholed trail that led to the ghost town.

The friends leapt out of the car and stared at the devastation before them. They were standing in the bottom of a mountain valley. Forested slopes towered on either side, but the barren valley bottom was covered with rocky rubble. Down the middle, a roaring torrent raced over rocks and boulders. It was contained between high gravel banks scattered with twisted beams, planks, and unidentifiable metal machinery. Set back from the river and scattered across the desolate landscape, several decrepit wooden buildings stood looking forlorn.

"What happened here?" asked Melissa. "It looks like a demolition site."

Willow leaned inside the car and came out clutching two sheets of paper. "These tell you all about it. I printed them off the Web yesterday." She started to read. "In 1900, Sandon was a booming mining city of 5000 inhabitants."

"That many?" said Melissa.

"In 1955, a massive flood swept through the centre of the town, washing entire buildings away," continued Willow.

Rick gazed respectfully at the foaming river, then bent down and threw in a chunk of wood. All three watched as it was tossed up over a standing wave and swept downstream.

"Awesome," said Melissa. "Let's explore."

"If there's someone in the buildings, maybe they can tell us where to find Boulder Bob," said Rick.

He and Willow ran towards the nearest building. Melissa followed more cautiously.

Sandon—from city to ghost town

A hundred years ago, Sandon was one of the biggest cities in British Columbia. Now it is a ghost town.

The 1891 discovery of galena (lead ore) west of Kaslo brought a rush of miners to the Kootenay Mountains. Five years later, 1500 people were living in the valley, which was so narrow that the main street was built over the creek. By 1897, Sandon was the first town in British Columbia entirely served by electricity. Next year it became a city, with two newspapers, seventeen hotels, and an opera house.

By 1900, when the population was 5000, a fire destroyed many of Sandon's buildings, and the city was rebuilt on a smaller scale. After ore prices dropped, the population declined, and by 1942 only 50 people called Sandon home. That was when the Canadian government moved 953 Japanese Canadians into Sandon's empty, rotting houses.

After the internees moved out in 1944, old houses collapsed or were demolished. In 1955, the creek flooded and destroyed more buildings.

Today, volunteers preserve some of Sandon's remaining buildings, and run the historic electric plant. Tourists enjoy visiting the isolated valley, once one of the biggest settlements in western Canada.

http://geoimages.berkeley.edu/GeoImages/QTVR/BCInterior/ KootenayLake.html

Dusty Malone swung the axe with a fluid movement. WHACK! The fir log fell neatly in four sections. Dusty wiped the sweat off his brow with his arm and bent to pick up the last log and place it on the chopping block.

"Not bad. Not a bad heap of wood, lad." Boulder Bob appeared in the cabin doorway. He hobbled over and clapped Dusty approvingly on the shoulder.

Dusty grinned, but inside he was seething. He had hoped to help for half an hour, then sit and have a chat with the old man. But Boulder was wily. It wasn't often someone came to help, and he took full advantage of it. The old fox had set Dusty up by the woodpile and tottered off to see a friend along the road at the Tin Cup Café.

Curses! A whole morning wasted splitting logs and loading them into the woodshed. And was Boulder Bob there to chat to? Not on your life.

WHACK. The last log flew apart and Dusty straightened up, and leaned the axe against the back wall of the tiny log cabin.

"Coffee's brewed." The old man turned and walked unsteadily inside.

Finally, a chance to talk. Dusty quickly stacked the remaining pieces and followed.

Despite the daylight, it was gloomy in the cabin. It was also hot and stuffy because the old man's only source of cooking was an ancient wood stove. A battered aluminum pan sat on top. As Dusty entered, the old man lifted it up and poured a thick dark brew into two dented aluminum mugs.

"Here, wet your whistle," Boulder Bob ordered, thrusting a mug towards Dusty and waving him into a sagging armchair.

Dusty sank into the armchair's depths and stretched out his legs. He lifted the mug in a salute. "Thanks." He thirstily gulped but spluttered as the strong, bitter liquid hit his throat.

"Jeez, Bob, this stuff's powerful enough to melt silver."

The old man cackled as he shuffled over to the table and spooned sugar into his coffee and stirred. "Aw, drink up. It'll put hairs on your chest. This is proper sourdough coffee. Me and Tommy drank it all the time. Never did us any harm. Kept the cold out."

The old man sat at the table, slurping his coffee.

Dusty sipped more cautiously, cleared his throat, and attempted to break the silence.

"Who was Tommy? A mate?"

Boulder Bob nodded. "The best mate a man could have. Him and me were partners."

Dusty felt the hair rise on the back of his neck. This was it. The first time he'd heard of a partner of Boulder Bob's called Tommy.

"When was this, Boulder? A long time ago?"

Boulder Bob gave a rusty chuckle. "Long before your time, lad." He looked wonderingly around the cabin.

"Been here sixty years. Don't seem like it. Seems like yesterday I come up prospecting."

"Did you come with Tommy?" asked Dusty, casually lifting his mug to take another sip.

Boulder Bob grinned. "Could say so. Now *he'd* say he'd come with me. That'd be the truth of it." He sighed. "Always one for the truth, Tommy."

"Was Tommy with you when you found the silver boulder?" asked Dusty, grinning lazily.

In an instant the mood changed. Boulder Bob's face mottled angrily. He stood up, grasping the edge of the table with one hand and waving his other in a fist at Dusty. "You never give up, do you, Malone? That's what all this was about, wasn't it? The boulder!" He snorted. "Help indeed."

Boulder Bob shuffled to the open doorway and fiddled behind it. He came out brandishing a broom. "Get on your way. You're just as meddlesome as your grandpappy. Get out before I sweeps you out with the trash!"

Boulder started sweeping the floor vigorously, raising a flurry of dust and banging Dusty's feet and legs.

"You're a crazy old coot!" Dusty yelled as he sprang from the chair and tried to dodge the broom. "I'll fix you. This is assault. I'll get you locked up again."

Boulder swept faster, making Dusty leap and skip out of the doorway to avoid being hit.

"Yeah, I'll fix you good. I'll find the silver boulder if it's the last thing I do!" shouted Dusty as he started down the path. He turned to shake his fist at the old man.

Boulder lifted the broom and pushed him in the chest. Dusty fell flat on his back.

Boulder Bob cackled as startled customers emerged from the Tin Cup Café and three young people in the distance stopped and stared.

"'Tain't nothin'. Just sweepin' out vermin, getting rid of the trash!" Boulder called.

A burly man walked over to Boulder and gently pried the broom from his grasp. "No threatening people, Boulder. Let the man go in peace."

Embarrassed, Dusty scrambled to his feet, headed for the nearest bushes, and disappeared from view.

Boulder looked defiantly around at the disapproving faces. "A man has a right to rid his place of trash," he muttered, and slowly and unsteadily returned to the cabin.

"Holy cow. If that's Boulder Bob, I'm outta here." Rick's eyes were as big as saucers.

"Was that Dusty running away?" asked Willow.

"Looked like him. I saw a red headband." Melissa sighed. "Now what?"

"The old man scared you, eh?" The burly man who'd confiscated Boulder Bob's broom came striding down the track towards them.

Melissa, Rick, and Willow nodded.

"Well, I thought I'd better come reassure you." The man gestured back at the cabin. "His name is Boulder Bob. He really is harmless. He's a crusty ninety-year-old

76

who's totally independent and doesn't tolerate fools."
The man smiled. "Were you coming to the Tin Cup Café?
I'll walk you up there if you're scared to pass the cabin
on your own."

"No thanks," said Melissa hurriedly. "I think we'll leave.
Actually a friend had sent us to meet Boulder Bob, but
I don't think we'll bother. Thanks anyway." She turned
to go.

"Hold on. Who sent you?"

"Captain Olund."

"Then that settles it. You should see old Boulder. He
rarely gets visitors, and the captain wouldn't have sent
you if it wasn't important." The man raised his voice.
"Hey, Boulder…someone to see you."

"If it's the police or welfare, I ain't coming out." Boulder's
shaky voice emerged from the depths of the cabin.

"It's neither, Boulder. It's some nice youngsters Captain
Olund sent along. You've scared them half to death."

Boulder's face appeared in the doorway. He glared
defiantly at Willow, Rick, and Melissa. "I don't know
them," he said flatly and started to retreat.

Melissa spoke up courageously. "Excuse me, sir." Her
voice came out all squeaky, so she cleared her throat and
tried again. "You don't know me, sir, but I think you and
my grandfather knew each other."

Boulder Bob turned again and peered into the sunshine.

"That is…if you are Mr. Robert McKenzie?" Melissa's
voice died away.

"Well, I never." Boulder Bob scratched his head and hobbled along the trail towards them. "Ain't heard that fancy label since I was in court." He stopped in front of them. "So who's your grandfather, girl?" He squinted at Melissa's face. "Japanese, are you?"

Melissa stepped back uncomfortably. "Yes. I'm Melissa Tomi. My grandfather, Nobu Tomi, lived here during the war."

Boulder Bob stared at them for a moment, then to everyone's surprise, his eyes slowly filled with tears. "Tommy...Tommy," he repeated softly. "You're Tommy's granddaughter. He didn't forget me after all...You better come inside."

CHAPTER NINE

Melissa, Willow, and Rick crowded into the little cabin. Boulder Bob blew his nose loudly, started to busy himself at the stove, then stopped. "Guess you young 'uns don't drink coffee?"

"No," Willow and Rick admitted.

Boulder pointed them towards the two sagging armchairs. He poured a fresh cup for himself and one for Melissa and walked to the table. He pulled out a chair for Melissa and sat down on the other with a dull thump. "Tommy's granddaughter. After all this time. Well, I'll be darned."

Melissa opened her purse, pulled out the photo and journal, and pushed them across to Boulder Bob.

Boulder picked up the photo and squinted at it. "That's Tommy." He placed the photo reverently on the table and gently stroked the journal's leather cover. "Dead, ain't he?"

"Yes," Melissa whispered. "Two months ago."

Boulder gently touched the journal again. "Yup. Tommy wouldn't let anyone look at this if he was alive." He grinned.

"Not that it mattered, the old dodger wrote in Japanese." He cackled. "Back to front and up and down. Now how was anyone going to figure that out, eh?" Boulder fell silent and gazed thoughtfully into space.

"Always wondered why he didn't come back," he muttered eventually.

"He thought you were in jail," Melissa said uncomfortably. "His family was taken from Sandon down to Kaslo. They were sent to Alberta before you came up for trial. It always bothered him that he wasn't allowed to send you a message."

"Yup. They had to put up with all kinds of rules." Boulder blew his nose noisily. "He wouldn't be allowed to see me and he wouldn't be allowed to write me. We weren't supposed to be friendly with enemy aliens, see." Boulder snorted in derision. "Enemy aliens! Tommy and me were mates. He was the best mate I ever had." He fell silent again, then looked embarrassed. "I should have written, but I can't. Can't read or write." He looked at Melissa. "Guess he never heard what happened at the trial."

"He thought you'd be in jail for life," said Melissa.

"So did I, so did I." Boulder peered around at Willow and Rick sitting silently in the chairs. "I killed a man, see. Didn't mean to, but that's what I did. Got two years. Would have been more but folks in town testified, see. They told the judge all about Meddlesome Malone. He filled his name in on our claim forms. Thought I wouldn't know. Me not having any schooling, see." Boulder snorted angrily. "I could recognize initials though. I ain't daft. R for Robert. It weren't there."

He turned back to Melissa. "Never meant to kill Meddlesome, just wanted to bang some sense into 'im. He tumbled downstairs and broke his neck. Tried to rip me and Tommy off, see. Tried to claim the boulder for himself."

"So the story about the silver boulder is true. There really is one?" said Willow excitedly.

"There's a boulder, all right. Full of silver and bigger than the lot of us, Tommy said. He found it, but I ain't seen it. Tommy said he'd share it with me but I weren't going to pinch his claim. After I got out of jail, the whole town watched me like a hawk. Some of 'em even followed me."

Boulder chuckled. "I fixed 'em though. Never went lookin' and never breathed a word." He smiled sadly. "Tommy said he'd come back, and we'd both go and get it one day."

Melissa groaned with disappointment. "So you don't know where it is?"

"Don't put words in my mouth, girl," Boulder said sharply. "If you've got the journal, you've got your grandfather's half of the map."

Melissa looked up at him, her eyes sparkling. She opened the journal to the middle and showed Boulder.

Boulder pushed his chair back and shuffled over to a cupboard. He opened the door and creakily tried to reach the top shelf but couldn't do it. "Hey, boy."

He pointed to Rick. "Stand on a chair and reach up there for me, eh?"

Rick moved the chair from the table, stood it in front of the cupboard, and climbed up.

"Right at the back, on the top shelf. There's an old can. Bring it down."

Rick stretched his arm as far as it could reach into the murky depths of the cupboard. He groped around until his fingers contacted a metal box. He pulled it out and handed it to Boulder Bob.

As he turned and stepped off the chair, Rick glimpsed a movement outside the open back window. Someone was crouching in the bushes below the window. Someone was listening!

Rick pointed and opened his mouth to speak, but Boulder Bob had already noticed.

Boulder laid his finger on his lips and motioned first to Rick and then to the mystified girls to follow him.

Rick whispered, "Someone's eavesdropping."

Willow and Melissa caught on. They tiptoed into the kitchen. Boulder gestured towards a tin bath half full of cold soapy water sitting on the floor. He mimed lifting it up and pouring it out the window.

With big grins Willow, Rick, and Melissa bent down and lifted the bath to window height.

"One, two, *three*," mouthed Boulder.

The cold water shot out of the window and drenched the figure crouched beneath.

With a yelp, Dusty shot to his feet and raced into the bushes again, leaving Boulder and Melissa roaring with laughter as Rick and Willow gleefully slapped each other's hands.

Boulder rubbed his hands together in childlike delight. "That fixed Meddlesome Malone Junior. Now, let's look in my can."

Everyone crowded around the table. Boulder's box was a faded but still elegant old can of Japanese green tea.

"Your grandmother gave me this the Christmas yer dad was born," Boulder explained to Melissa. "They lived with me then."

"In here? But it's tiny! How could three people and a baby fit in here?" Melissa looked around in wonder.

Boulder chuckled. "This was luxury compared to what they were allotted." He shook his head. "No better than a chicken coop was what they got. Walls full of gaps, no heat, and snow blowing in. I wouldn't have put a dog in there until it was fixed up. Let alone folks."

He gently tapped the baby in the photo, still lying on the table. "She was expecting, see, and wasn't well. Had to help her. She was such a little bitty thing." Boulder eyed Melissa. "You're twice her size. Got her hair though."

He lifted the lid of the tea can and wrinkled his nose at the musty leaves inside. "I never did get the taste for this, but your grandmother thought she was giving me a real treat. Never had the heart to tell her."

Boulder stuck a finger and thumb into the tea, felt around, and pulled out a tattered old piece of paper.

"This was our security, Tommy and me. We each had half the map, and if other folks found it? Well, neither half made sense on its own."

With trembling fingers, Melissa laid the two halves together. Suddenly everything was clear. The lake, Kaslo, and a morass of wiggly lines were on Boulder's half. They matched up exactly with the wiggly lines and the place marked with an X on Melissa's half.

>>>>>>>>>>>>>>> **The desire for silver** <<<<<<<<<<<<<

 "So great is the desire for silver, that for the gain thereof men endure any pains," said an early miner.

Silver is easily worked and has a beautiful shiny surface that can be highly polished. It has been used for necklaces for princesses, goblets for banquets, and chalices for church.

Silver was used first for pennies, and later nickels, dimes, and quarters. Silver is now too valuable for coins, so they are made of nickel alloys.

Today silver is still used for ornaments, but also turns up in the most surprising places. Silver is in the film you put in your camera, in electronic equipment, and may even be in fillings in your teeth.

www.infoplease.com/ipd/A0653709.html

>>><<<<<<<<<<<<<<<<<<<<<<<<<<<<<<<<<<<<<<<<<<<<

She ran her finger down from the X. "Are all these creeks running into the lake?"

"Yup." Boulder placed his finger on the map. "I reckon this 'ere is Mosquito Creek. The bugs there are terrible. But your grandfather gave it a fancy name. He could be kinda poetic sometimes. He called it Reflection Creek."

Willow nudged Rick. "The haiku," she whispered.

Boulder leaned towards Melissa. His eyes twinkled brightly under his bushy eyebrows. "SO?" he challenged.

Melissa shrugged.

"So?" Boulder asked once more. "Whatcha gonna do?"

Melissa broke into a wide grin. "Why, go there and find the boulder, of course! Want to come?"

The old man shuffled to his cupboard and rummaged along the bottom shelf. He shuffled back and dropped four old metal stakes in the middle of the table. "I'm ready," he grunted.

Rick and Willow whooped with delight. The old man beckoned everyone forward. "Now if we're gonna be prospectors, here's what we gotta do."

They put their heads together and plotted.

CHAPTER TEN

Hidden in an overgrown trail, Dusty Malone sat in his pickup and watched angrily. The three young people hoisted Boulder Bob into the back seat of Melissa's 4x4. There was a lot of laughter as Boulder hurled spicy curses at his stiff legs.

Dusty gripped the steering wheel. "Doggone kids," he muttered. "Gotta follow them. Where they go I'm goin'. Glue, that's what I'll be. Thick sticky glue stuck tight to their trail."

Thunder echoed through the valley, and a large raindrop plopped on the windshield. Dusty grinned nastily. "Roll on, rain. Let's have a big storm. They'll be so busy dealing with the bad roads, they won't notice me behind them."

The thunder clapped again. Willow and Rick looked up anxiously. Blue-black storm clouds were gathering over-head, obscuring the mountaintops. The air felt hot and heavy.

"Feels like a big storm," Willow muttered uneasily.

She didn't like storms. The electrically charged air made her head ache.

Rick stood on the riverbank. "Am I imagining things, or is the river higher?"

"Yer right." Boulder hung out of the 4x4's window to look. "Bin raining in the mountains. The river's swollen." He laughed. "That ol' river might bust its bank again. There's lots of snow in the mountains, see. The sun melts it, an' down it all comes in one big rush. Add heavy rain, me boy-oh, and you gets flash floods."

The rain started in earnest and the kids scrambled into the car. "Time to go," Melissa sang out, pulling onto the gravel road.

"Whoa boy," cackled Boulder as the car slipped in an instant mud slick, then bucked as it hit a pothole.

In seconds, the rain went from heavy to torrential and beat deafeningly on the roof. The windshield wipers struggled to keep up.

"This isn't a lot of fun," said Melissa after a few minutes. "I think I'd better pull off until the rain eases. Can you look for a space by the road, Willow?"

The rain sheeted down Willow's window, so she opened it to see out.

"Jeez, thanks." Rick and Boulder both were hit full blast as the water swept in.

"Sorry, guys." Willow rolled the window back up.

"Melissa, use the four-wheel drive and boot it," advised Rick.

"Yup. Waiting's no good," agreed Boulder. "This road's a regular mud hole in a storm. Folks is always being hauled out. Do what the lad suggests. Boot it." He cackled again.

Melissa's hands tightened on the wheel. She looked worried. The car slipped sideways and bucked over a large rock.

"What's the problem?" asked Rick. "Why don't you use the four-wheel drive?"

There was a slight pause. "I can't remember how to work it," admitted Melissa. "I've never used it."

"No sweat." Rick leaned forward and pointed over her shoulder. "Press that button to engage the wheel hubs, then move the gears into four-wheel-drive mode. Uncle Joe showed me on his."

"I'll try." Melissa tentatively adjusted the drive. The sound of the engine changed and immediately the wheels gripped.

"NOW BOOT IT!" came the cry from the back seat.

Melissa drove through the rain, gravel, and mud until, accompanied by cheers, she reached the highway.

No one sang on the drive down to Kaslo. The highway was a shock—its condition was almost as bad as the gravel road. The torrential rain continued and the storm grew wilder. Wind buffeted the 4x4, and branches were blown across the road. The river, swelling by the minute, roared alongside, spilling over the road in places, tugging at their wheels.

Melissa jutted out her chin and concentrated on making slow, steady progress. The 4x4 lived up to the challenge.

Rick and Boulder Bob swapped disaster stories in the back seat and Willow chewed her thumb nervously in the front. Everyone watched for the welcoming signs of Kaslo.

No one seemed to notice Dusty's yellow pickup following them.

"Where should we take you?" Melissa asked Boulder when they reached Front Street.

"Drop me at the *Moyie*. I'll be stayin' with the captain tonight."

"I'll wait and give you both a lift if you like," Melissa offered. "You'll get soaked if you try to walk anywhere."

"Aw, someone always looks after us." Boulder grinned as he eased himself out of the 4x4. "I'll see you all here tomorrow. Eh?" He staggered against the wind, then tottered into the shelter of the visitor centre.

They drove up to the Langham.

"Thank goodness you're back." A flustered Shari met everyone at the door and led the way up to their office. "We're driving to Nelson. Immediately."

"In this storm?" asked Willow disbelievingly.

"We've got the chance to give a presentation about the film program to a funding agency there," Shari continued. "We'll stay overnight. We'll take the school's mini-van and pick up some equipment on the way back tomorrow morning."

"Why can't Willow and I stay if you're not taking the bus?" asked Rick.

"I'm not leaving you on your own overnight," said Shari flatly. "Come on. There isn't much time."

Willow and Rick rolled their eyes and turned to thank Melissa.

"Er, could I help?" Melissa followed Shari into the office. "Um…I mean…I don't mind staying with Rick and Willow."

Willow immediately crossed her fingers behind her back. "Please say yes, please say yes, please say yes," she chanted under her breath.

"What? Overnight?" asked Shari.

"Yes. Say yes," interrupted Willow eagerly.

"Aren't you sick of them by now?" Shari asked, a small line of concern between her brows.

"We had a great time. We were going to ask about going on another trip tomorrow. Up to Mosquito Creek. So no, I don't mind staying." Melissa grinned. "We could rent a movie."

"What do you think, Marty?"

"Brave woman…you sure?"

Melissa laughed. "I'm sure."

"Magnificent. We owe you, Melissa." Marty wrote rapidly on a card and passed it to Melissa. "Here are Mrs. Dreger's phone numbers at home and at work. She's the secretary here. Phone her if there's an emergency. She'll know how to help, or how to get hold of us in Nelson."

Marty slapped down two $20 bills. "Have a good supper. We'll see you around lunchtime tomorrow."

Giving his kids a bear hug, Marty swept out, dragging Shari behind him. They waved madly and jumped in the Arts School van, driving off in a flurry of spray from the puddles.

"Whew," Melissa gasped. "Does your family always make decisions like that?"

"Always." Willow nodded.

"It's split-second timing," agreed Rick. "You get used to it."

"Okay." Melissa looked at her charges. "I'm tired from all the driving. It was pretty hairy. Let's veg out tonight."

"Pizza and movies?" suggested Willow.

"Lots of movies," agreed Rick as they clattered downstairs. "Then we each get something we like."

"Nothing with Arnold Schwarzenegger in, okay?"

"Only if *you* promise not to get chick flicks."

Arguing amiably, the three of them left the Langham.

Dusty Malone left his hiding place in the Langham's exhibit room. He watched from the shadow of the doorway as the kids climbed into the 4x4 and drove towards the video store. "Easy as pie." He grinned. "It's at Mosquito Creek. Those clear young voices might as well have announced it from the rooftop."

Dusty dashed through the rain and into his pickup. "First light, I'm outta here. By the time they get to Mosquito Creek, the silver boulder will be staked!"

CHAPTER 11

The storm showed no sign of abating. It battered Kaslo, bringing down trees, scattering roof tiles, and whipping the lake into a frenzy. The rising lake covered the beach, and the waves broke against the bank. Spray swirled across Front Street.

The big blue bus was surrounded by a howling darkness.

"I hope Mom and Dad are okay—this storm is awful." Willow was tightly curled in an afghan on the bench seat.

"They'll be fine. They should be there by now. Besides, it's probably not storming in Nelson," Melissa comforted her.

Rick squatted in front of the TV. "The storm's interfering with reception. I can't get a good picture," he grumbled. "This is crazy. Let's go eat."

Melissa parked the 4x4 near the *Moyie* and everyone got out.

"Look at the waves! They're almost reaching the *Moyie's* hull." Rick's words were swallowed by the wind.

The wind was so strong that even street lights swayed disconcertingly, the wavering pools of light making the darkness seem even blacker. Rick and Willow jammed on their hats, and ran across the deserted road to the pizza parlour. Melissa's umbrella blew inside out, so she shut it quickly. She ran across the road into the café.

"Here comes the drowned rat," observed Rick.

Melissa grinned and flicked the drip from a strand of wet hair in his direction.

Lightning forked through the sky and an enormous thunder clap made the little café shake on its foundations.

"Better order fast." A teenage boy in faded jeans slapped three menus on the table. "The power might go."

"What do you mean?" asked Willow.

"In the storm." The boy looked from one to the other and realized no one understood. "If a tree falls on the power lines, we'll have a blackout. It's always happening."

"That would make it hard to read the menus." Melissa opened hers. "What would we do, eat by candlelight?"

"No power, no pizza. The oven's electric. Call me when you're ready."

"Call you what?" grinned Willow.

"My name's Paul. I'll be your waiter this evening," he said. "And your cook. And your dish washer," he added flatly.

"Let's order. I'm starving." Rick looked across at Melissa and Willow. "Zippo pineapple and anchovies, okay?"

"Meat and cheese?" Willow looked at Melissa.

"Green pepper?" Melissa asked. The gagging reflexes answered her. "Got ya. Ham, salami, and pepperoni, and three colas?"

Rick and Willow nodded.

Paul disappeared in the back.

The warmth of the café made everyone drowsy. They sat silently watching the runnels of rain on the window.

Finally, Willow roused out of her stupor. "Melissa, check for a haiku in your grandfather's journal." She unzipped her fanny pack and pulled out the haiku Rick had discovered on the Net.

Melissa pulled the diary out of her purse and turned the small pages. She paused. "This looks like a poem." She gazed at the Japanese words thoughtfully. "It says something like 'the gift of moonlight,' then there is a character I don't understand."

"Is there another gift?" asked Willow eagerly.

Melissa concentrated. "Could be… 'a gift from the earth' —does that make sense?"

"The silver boulder," yawned Rick.

"What?" Melissa and Willow stared at him.

"The silver boulder. It's a gift from the earth."

"That's it. You're brilliant, Rick. Not bad for a younger brother."

Rick stuck his tongue out. "Told you it was written by Melissa's grandfather."

"Then it's gotta be a clue about the silver boulder.

Let's look." Willow spread the printed poem on the table
for Melissa to see.

> Moonlight, gift from sky.
> Cedar-wrapped rock, gift from earth.
> Each reflecting each.
> —Tomi

Melissa's face flushed with excitement. "Moonlight is
silver, and if the rock is also silver, then each reflects each.
Grandfather wrote this? WOW!"

"I don't get the part about the cedar wrapping, though,"
Rick wondered. "That's weird."

"I bet that's the hidden clue," said Willow with conviction. "I bet, if we can solve 'cedar-wrapped rock,' we've
found the boulder."

Rick suddenly pressed his nose to the window. "That's
strange."

"What is?" asked Willow with a yawn.

"There was a light flickering opposite…" He peered
through the streaming glass again.

"The *Moyie's* across the street. It must have been a reflection from the streetlights," Willow suggested.

"Guess so." Rick slumped back in his chair.

Silently Paul appeared and placed the drinks on the
table. One of them wobbled and slopped. Melissa quickly
grabbed the poem and stowed it in her purse. The smell
of cooking pizza began to drift through the restaurant.

A particularly strong buffet of wind struck the building. As it shuddered, the lights flickered.

"Uh-oh." Three pairs of eyes flew to the ceiling fixtures, but nothing else happened and everyone relaxed.

Paul visited the kitchen and returned with two candles. "Just in case," he muttered. "I'll get some matches. Pizza won't be long."

They sat sleepily sipping drinks.

Willow yawned again and her eyes drooped. Then they snapped wide open. "What if it's still stormy tomorrow?"

Melissa looked horrified.

"It won't be," Rick said with conviction. "Dad says thunderstorms blow themselves out."

The delicious aroma of bubbling cheese made everyone look expectantly towards the kitchen. A flash of lightning, as brilliant as the midday sun, backlit Paul carrying their pizza.

CRACK. The thunder was right overhead.

Everything went black.

A body bumped into furniture. Then came a curse, a slither, and the clatter of metal rolling across the floor. Paul groaned.

Several clicks and a cigarette lighter flamed.

Paul carefully made his way across the café to their table. He lit the candles and looked at his three customers.

"Er...sorry about your pizza." He lifted one of the candles to illuminate the restaurant.

A chair leaned against a table, which was littered with

pieces of pizza. A couple more were on the floor along with the plate.

Melissa surveyed the wreckage. "The power's out. No more pizza, eh?"

Paul nodded glumly.

"Well, I'm starving." Rick pushed his chair back and picked up his plate. He walked over to the table, peeled off several slices of pizza, placed them on the plate and returned.

"Anyone else?" He began to eat.

Willow made a face, then looked across at their waiter. "When will the power come back on?"

"Tomorrow."

Changing her mind, Willow reached for a slice of pizza and took a bite. "It tastes okay," she said to Melissa.

Reluctantly, Melissa took a piece. "I guess this is supper," she sighed.

Paul vanished with one candle, then reappeared a few minutes later. One by one, he lit several candles and arranged them around the café.

Willow nodded in approval. "Pretty."

Next, he rustled behind the counter and returned to their table clutching something to his chest. "Your supper's on the house," he explained, dropping six bags of chips in the middle. "And there's apple pie if you want it."

"Right on," said Rick.

Melissa brightened. "Thanks," she said. "We want it!"

The patched-up meal was soon over. The three friends huddled in the café's doorway and looked up and down Front Street. No lights were visible.

"The whole town's lost power." Willow shuddered. "Creepy. It's totally deserted, as if we're the only people here."

They ran across the wet road, the wind almost knocking them off their feet. "Yay, some moonlight," Melissa cheered quietly. "And the rain's stopped."

"Then why am I still getting wet?" Willow wiped a fresh drip off her nose.

"The wind's blowing the tops off the waves. The lake has really risen. You can hear the waves hitting the *Moyie*." Rick paused and cocked his head. "Listen."

But Willow clutched his arm and pointed towards the looming black mass of the sternwheeler. "Rick. Over there."

"What?"

"A flickering light. A flickering flame on the *Moyie*." Willow stood still. "Do you think it was hit by lightning? Is it on fire?"

All three of them stared into the darkness, but they couldn't see anything.

"Weird! If it was a fire you'd think we'd keep seeing it. Better check it out." Rick gripped the low fence around the *Moyie* and swung his leg over.

"Don't!" Willow tried to grab his arm. "There's a drop through the bushes on the other side."

Too late. Melissa and Willow heard Rick slither down through the darkness to land with a thud on the walkway.

"You okay?" Melissa called worriedly.

"Yeah. Just scratched. Now shut up. What if it's burglars?"

"Rick, come back. We'll get the police." Melissa was frantic. "You can't face burglars on your own."

"What if it's the ghost!" Willow's sibilant whisper cut through the night. Then she gave a frightened squeak.

The cargo door of the *Moyie* slowly creaked open, and a shadowy figure holding a flashlight materialized.

The beam of light caught Rick and held him fast.

"What in tarnation's going on?" boomed a voice.

CHAPTER TWELVE

"Captain Olund, thank goodness!" Willow's voice called through the darkness.

The flashlight beam left Rick and travelled up the bank. It paused on Willow's and Melissa's white faces looking down over the bushes.

"Captain Olund. It's us. Rick, Willow, and Melissa," Willow continued.

The beam moved away and slid down to Rick again. "So it is…what in heaven's name are you up to?" asked the captain gruffly.

"We saw a flickering light—an'—an' thought there might be a fire," Rick stuttered with relief.

"Or burglars," Melissa's voice floated down.

"Or the ghost." Willow's voice had a shaky giggle.

"So—so—I came down to check it out," Rick finished in a rush.

"Hmph," the captain snorted. "You'd better come aboard. You too." He trained the flashlight beam on the two girls, then moved it farther along the bank. "There's some steps over there. Try not to bring the shrubbery down with you."

Willow and Melissa negotiated the bank and arrived safely on the landing stage.

Everyone slid inside the cargo door. Captain Olund slammed it shut.

"'T'ain't Meddlesome's ghost walkin' again, is it?" asked a quavery voice from the shadows. Boulder appeared holding a candle.

"No, it's those kids. Your candle flame scared them. I told you not to use a candle. They're a fire hazard," the captain muttered crossly. "And don't drop wax. The staff will have a fit."

Melissa looked from one old man to the other. "So that's why you didn't need me to run you anywhere, Boulder. You're sleeping on board, with the captain. He lives here."

The cargo deck in daylight was a maze of interesting equipment. On a stormy night, in a power outage, it was scary. The captain walked in front, his flashlight beam highlighting obstacles that faded into the darkness as he moved forward. Willow, Rick, and Melissa shuffled in single file, hands on each other's shoulders. Boulder brought up the rear. His candle flickered constantly, sending long eerie shadows dancing around them. No one could talk over the constant noise of waves pounding the hull.

They finally reached the saloon and relaxed in the comfortable chairs. Boulder's candle, stuck on a saucer, threw a golden glow on their faces.

"This is more like it. I likes a bit of company." Boulder rubbed his hands together gleefully. "Who's for a friendly hand of poker?" He pulled a pack of worn cards from his pocket and shuffled them with amazing dexterity.

"Put 'em away. You can't fleece kids," Captain Olund ordered.

"Would I do that?" Boulder's voice had a querulous note.

"Aw, you've won every game for years." The captain's eyes twinkled in the candlelight. "He's won more money at poker than he ever found prospecting."

The youngsters giggled.

"Yup. Better odds most times," Boulder agreed.

A loud bang made everyone jump. The young people glanced around uneasily.

"The storm's driven a log against the hull. She's a sturdy boat, though. Nothing to worry about," the captain reassured them.

"Does anyone know you're living here?" asked Rick.

The captain laughed. "It's a small town. It would be pretty hard to keep a secret like that. No, I've lived here for years." He looked around fondly. "Someone had to keep an eye on the old *Moyie* when she was first beached. I wasn't about to see her broken up by vandals, so I moved in. When she became a museum, I just kinda stayed on. It suited everyone to have a built-in security system." He laughed again. "I'm so used to the old wooden bunk, I'd find it impossible to sleep in a regular bed."

Boulder bent down, picked up the flashlight, and shuffled off into the darkness. He reappeared with a couple of bottles tucked under his arm and several cups dangling from his fingers. He dumped everything on the table with a clatter.

"What's your pleasure, Captain?"

"The usual."

Boulder poured some rye whisky in two of the cups and passed one over to Captain Olund. He pushed the other bottle towards Willow. "This is more to your likin'."

It was a bottle of ginger ale. Willow grinned and poured some out for Melissa, Rick, and herself.

"Remember the poker game that went on nonstop for three weeks?" Boulder asked the captain.

"Three weeks?" said Melissa. "Really?"

The captain nodded. "It's true, one ship had a game that lasted nearly a month. The men would take over one another's hands, eh. As passengers were dropped off, others joined in. Then when we picked the first one up on the return journey, he'd take over again. Mind you, there were a few arguments about how hands should have been played."

"Our game only quit when Crazy Pete tried to stake his mine," chuckled Boulder. "Scotty MacDonald reminded Pete he'd already lost it in a game in Nelson the week before. Fine old ruckus that was."

"Then there were the races," the captain mused.

"Races around the deck?" asked Rick.

"Lordy no, races up the lake. We'd race the ships. There were several sternwheelers then. We'd load with fuel, get a good head of steam, and let her rip. The paddle would thrash the water so fast the whole ship would shudder and groan. Glasses and plates jumped right off the shelves."

"I liked the balls on a summer evenin' meself." Boulder smiled in recollection. "The town band played on the

>>>>>>>>> **Sternwheeler excursions** <<<<<<<<<

Sternwheelers were working boats, carrying passengers and freight. But occasionally they brought local residents together for a pleasure trip, providing a break from the grind of mining or farming.

Adults took shopping trips to local towns or enjoyed special moonlight dance cruises. Children travelled free to Sunday school picnics.

For outings, the *Moyie* would be decorated with flags and tree branches. The crew wore their best uniforms, and the passengers dressed in their finest. Often a band played on deck as the boat sailed up the lake. For dances, the furniture in the saloon was pushed aside, and a pianist and fiddler would play. When the crowd was big and the evening lively, extra timbers would be fixed under the deck, for the dancers "got to stomping pretty good."

>>><<<<<<<<<<<<<<<<<<<<<<<<<<<<<<<<<<<<<<<<<

deck, see. We'd spit 'n polish our boots, an' wear our best duds. There were some mighty fine young ladies waltzing around here. Real pretty in their dresses and gewgaws."

The stories continued, tumbling out one after the other. The two old-timers had never had such an appreciative audience.

Suddenly a jarring thud made the *Moyie* shudder.

Boulder and the captain clambered to their feet.

Another shudder ran through the boat, and she rocked from side to side.

Everyone gasped and grabbed the table to steady themselves. The ginger ale bottle fell off and rolled over the floor.

"What's happening?" asked Rick, his voice scared.

The boat rocked again. There were several crashes as plates and ornaments tumbled off cabin shelves, and something scraped along the hull.

The captain stood upright, feet apart. "Well, well, well. I haven't heard that noise for a long time. If I'm not much mistaken, the lake's risen so high we're afloat. She's lifted right out of the cradle and is scraping alongside the wharf."

Willow, Rick, and Melissa leapt from their chairs and ran unsteadily across the gently rocking floor to the windows. They peered into the blackness but couldn't see anything.

Boulder cackled. "I told 'em...I told 'em. One of these days, I said, we'll have another flood like the one in 1894.

My grandpappy told me the lake rose over thirty feet then. I told 'em...I told 'em. But no one listens to old Boulder Bob."

Once again the *Moyie* lurched sideways beneath their feet.

"Stay here," the captain ordered. "I'm going on deck to see what's happening."

"Oh no! We're going to be shipwrecked!" Melissa moaned.

"Come on, Willow. Let's see if we can jump to shore and get help."

Rick and Willow blundered through the dim cabin after Captain Olund. The moon gleamed between the clouds scudding across the sky. The wind blew hard in their faces as they hung over the rails. A growing gap of water glimmered between the side of the bobbing *Moyie* and the receding black mass of the land.

"How big a gap do you think it is, Willow?"

"Dunno. It's too dark to judge."

"Don't be thinking of jumping. The wind's blowing us out into the lake too fast," said the captain behind them.

"So what *are* we supposed to do?" asked Willow. "Just wait until we get shipwrecked?"

Captain Olund grinned from ear to ear, his teeth glinting in the moonlight. "Seems like I'm a working captain again. How about signing on as crew?"

Prospectors find more good stories than they do mines.

In 1882, American Robert Sproule staked the "Big Ledge" across the lake from Kaslo. By law he had to work his claim through the summer, but he left for supplies when he had nothing to eat but flour.

An English miner, Thomas Hammill, declared the mine abandoned and staked it for himself. When Sproule returned, he found Hammill camped at the site. Legal battles left the rivals working side by side, until the day Hammill's body was found in the bush. Sproule was convicted of murder after a tense trial.

A little later, Eli Carpenter and John Seaton went prospecting together west of Kaslo. Carpenter had rich samples assayed (tested), but told Seaton they were worthless. Carpenter's plans to return secretly to the strike with another partner were overheard in a saloon. When Seaton learned this he raced back to the strike with new partners. By the time Carpenter arrived, Seaton had already staked the Noble Five Mine.

Once a tightrope walker in Barnum's circus, Carpenter later astonished the townsfolk when he stretched a high wire between two hotels on Sandon's Main Street and walked across, pausing to cook bacon and eggs in mid-air.

CHAPTER THIRTEEN

Despite the rocking of the deck, the saloon became a hive of activity. Captain Olund ordered everyone to look for candles, oil lamps, and lanterns.

"We're going to need lights down in the engine room until we can get the engine going."

"Aye aye, sir." Rick was in his element now that someone seemed to know what to do.

Melissa was a different story. She held her stomach and moaned softly.

"Don't tell me. The lass is seasick. Come on up with you. A bit of fresh air will fix that." The captain put his arm around her and they staggered to the doorway. He propped it open. Melissa took some deep breaths and leaned against the wall.

The ship heaved and wallowed in the waves. There was a smashing and banging as plates and dishes fell off shelves and loose objects rolled around the deck.

"What if we hit rocks?" Melissa whispered fearfully.

"We won't," Captain Olund stated. "There are no rocks

in the middle of the lake." He shone his flashlight on a framed map hanging on the wall. "The lake fills this long mountain valley. We're being blown straight down the middle. It's a big lake. We can be blown for miles without hitting land."

"But what if the wind changes again and blows us across…"

"Melissa, it's not going to happen," the captain replied firmly. "The mountains act like a funnel with the wind going up or down. If the wind changes, we'll be blown back towards Kaslo."

"Why can't we just start the engine and get back to Kaslo?" asked Willow. "You told us this ship was as good as the day she was built."

Everyone looked at the captain.

"Ah," he said. "There are two problems. We don't have much coal, and it's going to take over an hour's hard work to stoke up and get a head of steam."

"We'll help!" said Willow and Rick.

"The coal won't last long," the captain continued. "I've got to be sure of the best time to use it."

"What if the wind drops?" asked Melissa.

"No problem. We'll drift peacefully and catch some sleep. Kaslo will miss us as soon as it's light. Then some-one will come and tow us back."

"Tomorrow…We won't be rescued until tomorrow?" Melissa's voice trembled. "We were going to Mosquito Creek tomorrow."

"That old silver boulder ain't going nowhere." Boulder Bob patted her shoulder.

"But someone else might get there first," said Willow.

"Why? Who did you tell?" demanded Boulder.

"No one. It's just…" Willow's voice trailed off. She looked around the saloon. "I dunno…I feel we should be there."

"Me too." Melissa shivered. "Something is bugging me. A reason why we shouldn't wait."

"It's Meddlesome," muttered Boulder. "The old buzzard's walking again. He's still trying to get the boulder." He glanced fearfully around the flickering shadows of the saloon. No one argued with him.

It was a long, cold, exhausting night.

Melissa took the first watch. Terrified, she patrolled the decks, constantly checking that the *Moyie* wasn't blown too close to shore. Twice she had to lean over the rail to be sick, but she never told anyone. *If the wind changes and we are blown back to Kaslo, we could be smashed aground there,* she worried as she stared into the darkness.

Belowdecks, the two old men muttered to each other.

"This is a bad turn of events, Boulder," said Captain Olund. "We've gotta get those young folk back safely."

Boulder grunted. He'd worked on the steamships as a young man. He eyed the pipes and gave the joints a poke. "If them pipes give when we get a head of steam, it's gonna be nasty. Real nasty. Could scald someone to death, see."

Captain Olund checked the engines and the boiler and sighed. "Well, it's the best we can do. A body can't do more than that." He gave the pipes a gentle pat. "She's never let me down yet."

"Lets hope this ain't the first time," Boulder muttered uneasily.

Rick and Willow, roped to the side of the ship for safety, were hauling water. They were so wet they looked half drowned.

"How many more buckets do we need? My arms are killing me," grunted Willow as she leaned over the side to lower another fire bucket into the lake.

"Mine too," muttered Rick. "That old boiler is gigantic; the water we've hauled barely covers the bottom. I hope Boulder Bob and the captain can get the pump working." They heaved together on the rope and pulled another brimming bucket aboard.

"What if the engine won't work?" asked Rick anxiously.

"Don't even think about it," replied Willow.

Boulder Bob and the captain finally prepared the furnace to their satisfaction and left everything ready to fire her up.

The captain looked around at his worn and shivering crew. "We need blankets." He and Boulder Bob stripped their bunks, then got blankets from the museum displays and handed them out.

Swaddled and dry but still shivering, everyone sat out

the storm. The candlelight caught the whites of their eyes as they tried to hide their worries from one another.

Suddenly, Rick sat up straight. "Listen."

"What?" asked the captain groggily.

"I hear nuffin'," said Boulder.

"That's the point. There's nothing to hear. The wind and waves have dropped."

"Ain't silence beautiful," murmured Boulder.

"We'll be fine now. We're just drifting." Captain Olund sighed with relief. "Storm's over, better catch some sleep. Everyone happy if we divide the watches between us?"

"Sure, captain," came a soft chorus.

"I'll take a two-hour watch now while the rest of you get some sleep. Then I'll wake Boulder. He'll wake Rick and Willow. Then it's Melissa's turn again." He smiled across at her. "I'll probably be up by then anyway."

Wearily, Willow levered herself out of her chair. Dragging her blankets, she staggered sleepily to the Smoking Saloon and the bench seat running around the edge. She lay down.

"Good idea," muttered Rick. He and Melissa followed her example.

"G'night, Captain," whispered Willow as her eyes closed.

"Good night, crew. Well done."

Under the watchful eye of Captain Olund, the *Moyie* drifted slowly through the dark, peacefully riding the current in the middle of the lake.

Kaslo will never forget the year 1894. In February, a fire destroyed a major section of Front Street. The town started to rebuild, but before it was completed, another disaster came along.

Winter had brought an unusually heavy snowfall, followed by a cold, wet spring, then a sudden warm spell at the beginning of June. The snow in the mountains melted so quickly that Kootenay Lake rose 11 metres above normal—one day, it went up half a metre. The first floors of many houses in the lower town were submerged. When the Kaslo River burst its banks, other parts of town were flooded.

On June 3, a storm broke, and a fierce wind blew the lake into waves up to 3 metres tall. In town, so much sand was in the air that it was impossible to see across the street, and small stones rattled on buildings like rifle shots—even small dogs were blown away, some never to be seen again.

By the end of the storm, more than eighty houses had been demolished by the flood. It was nearly a week before the lake began to go down.

There have been other floods since, some almost as serious. Now the Duncan Dam controls lake levels.

www.wkpower.com/ (shows current levels of Kootenay Lake)

The June dawn coloured the sky with a faint pink glow. The mountains were dark shapes against it.

Boulder snored in his bunk. Rick and Willow were still splayed out in the Smoking Saloon. Melissa anxiously leaned against the deck railing. Not only was she worried about getting Rick and Willow home safely, but the nagging feeling about the silver boulder persisted.

The captain joined her. "It's going to be a lovely day." He patted the *Moyie's* deck rail proudly. "She rode the storm beautifully."

Melissa pointed to the shore. "Can you tell where we are yet?"

The captain peered at the line of mountains. "I need a little more light to see exactly. But I reckon we're about three miles from Kaslo."

Willow and Rick appeared, tousle-haired and sleepy-eyed, but otherwise looking none the worse for their adventure.

"Boulder's fixing something for breakfast," said Rick.

"If everyone is awake, I'll go down to light the furnace," said the captain. "It will take a good hour to get steam up. We can all eat while it's heating. We haven't drifted as far as I thought, so we might have enough coal to reach Kaslo."

Everyone was hungry, but there wasn't much for breakfast.

"I wasn't expecting visitors," Captain Olund apologized. "I usually eat at the café across the road." The bread and jam, cookies and apples soon disappeared, washed down with the last bottle of the ginger ale.

"Soon as we've got steam up, I'm making coffee," Boulder Bob announced. "'T'ain't right starting the day without coffee."

The sunrise was beautiful. As the sky became brighter and brighter, the mountaintops began to shine, first a pale pink, then a deeper peach; finally they flamed with a fiery orange glow. Suddenly the lake was awash with sunlight. It warmed everyone's sleep-chilled bodies and brought colour to their cheeks.

Boulder stretched. "Feels good bein' up with the sun."

"We're not the only early birds." Rick pointed to a truck driving along the lakeside.

Willow leaned over the deck railing. "Wonder if we could attract their attention." She waved both arms vigorously.

"Too far away to see you," the captain said.

"They can see the *Moyie* though."

"But unless you know the *Moyie*, we just look like an old boat on the lake," the captain pointed out. "But he could be coming from Kaslo."

Rick was still watching the truck, frowning. "Do you have binoculars or a telescope on board?" he asked.

Captain Olund disappeared into the cabin and reappeared with an old leather and brass telescope. He handed it to Rick.

"What is it?" asked Willow.

Rick rested the telescope on the rail and focused on the truck. "I don't believe it." He handed it to Willow. "Look."

Willow looked through. "Oh no...a yellow truck. Do you think it's Dusty?"

Rick nodded, his face serious.

"That's it. That's what's bugging me. A yellow truck followed us from Sandon yesterday. I meant to tell you, but the drive was so hairy I forgot." Melissa paced up and down. "We've *got* to get to Mosquito Creek."

"So what! Dusty Malone's always buzzin' into town," Boulder said.

"No, I saw the truck again when we went to the Langham. It was parked in a weird place. As though he was hiding it." Melissa was becoming more agitated.

"You think he followed us, don't you?" Willow said bluntly. "You're scared Dusty overheard us when we told Mom we wanted to go to Mosquito Creek."

Melissa nodded, her eyes full of misery.

Willow looked at the truck again, then turned back to the group. "I think Melissa is right. As we drove off, I noticed a man wearing a headband leaving the Langham."

"Dusty again!" said Rick.

Captain Olund watched the truck. "You think Dusty's heading to Mosquito Creek, eh? I reckon that's a couple of miles farther along the shore."

Melissa groaned. "I knew it. Dusty will get there first and stake the silver boulder."

"Hold on a minute." Willow was still looking through

the telescope. "The truck's stopped…Dusty's got out." Her voice rose. "The road's blocked. There's a fallen tree blocking the road."

"Right on," said Rick. But his voice died away as Willow frowned and flapped her hand at him.

She peered intently through the telescope. "He's going to the back of the pickup."

"Let me look." Rick tried to pull the telescope from Willow. She hung on tight. Rick reluctantly backed off.

"He's taken something from the truck…I can't see what it is."

A distinctive sound floated over the water.

"Chainsaw," said Boulder, nodding. "All the young prospectors carry 'em. He's got a chainsaw. That'll shift the tree."

Rick turned to the captain and saluted. "Permission to request change of destination, Sir."

Captain Olund looked at him with a twinkle in his eye. "Don't tell me, lad. You want the *Moyie* to race that truck to Mosquito Creek."

"With that tree blocking Dusty's way, we've got a fighting chance to beat him," Rick said with a grin.

Melissa's eyes shone.

Captain Olund turned his head. "What do you think, Boulder?"

Boulder Bob cackled. "Just like old times," he wheezed. "Bet you a hundred bucks it can't be done."

"You ain't got a hundred bucks, you old liar," Captain Olund retorted. "So let's do it anyway."

118

"YES!" Rick, Willow, and Melissa pounded each other's backs.

"Right, crew. All hands below deck. Boulder is chief engineer. Everything he says goes. Got it?"

"Got it, Captain!"

"He'll be in the pilothouse. You'll hear my orders through the speaking tube. All crew to their stations."

"Aye aye, Captain!"

The race was on.

CHAPTER FOURTEEN

Buzzzzzzzzzzz.

Feet apart, Dusty Malone stood on the giant spruce tree trunk. He shifted his weight and carefully guided his chainsaw through the last branch. The blade shrieked, and the branch fell. Dusty switched off and took a break.

"Good thing I got an early start. This is gonna take a while." He flexed his arms to relieve the muscles after holding the heavy chainsaw. "I just hope those interfering kids don't catch up with me," he muttered.

Then a thought crossed his mind. He jumped from the log and walked to the forest edge. *Yes!* A second tree had been damaged in the storm and was leaning badly. "A rope to the truck will pull that down," he chuckled. "Once I'm past this tree, I'll block the road behind me."

Dusty gazed out across the lake. "Jumping Jezebel. The *Moyie's* floated off in the flood." He contemplated driving back to Kaslo to raise the alarm. "Naw. She's safe enough drifting in the current." He went back to his chainsaw.

The hard work of the *Moyie's* scratch crew paid off. The cargo deck generator was running and a few dim lights were now operational in the engine room. The light helped everyone work faster.

Boulder Bob stiffly clambered around, releasing valves and directing Melissa how and when to move levers and gears.

Rick and Willow were stokers. It was a hot, dirty job—so hot they had stripped down to T-shirts. Bending and swinging, they constantly shovelled coal into the roaring furnace.

"How is it going down there?" A disembodied voice came through the speaking tube.

"Building steam nicely. Another ten minutes, Captain!" Boulder hollered back.

Rick and Willow rolled white eyes in their black faces, but doggedly kept on working. The sweat left light tracks through the coal dust covering their skin.

"Okay, Captain!" Boulder finally shouted. "We have a head of steam."

Willow and Rick leaned on their shovels, panting but smiling triumphantly.

"When I give the signal, start slowly. Make sure everything is easing in nicely. If anything breaks, shut her off."

"Aye aye, Captain!" bellowed Boulder. He turned towards his helpers. "Out of the way. On the double. This could be dangerous. Just hope like heck these blessed joints hold."

Melissa, Rick, and Willow raced to the far end of the ship and took cover behind boxes of cargo.

"Cross your fingers," Willow said.

Slowly and gently, Boulder Bob opened the valves.

Everyone held their breath.

No steam escaped from the old joints, and nothing exploded. There was just some hissing and clicking as the pipes heated up.

"Right! Back to the stokehole," came the bellow. "Keep on shovelling, you lily-livered weaklin's."

"Yes! It's gonna work!" Rick, Willow, and Melissa punched the air in triumph and ran laughing back to their stations.

High in his eyrie, Captain Henry Olund grasped the *Moyie*'s wheel. Never in his wildest dreams had he thought the two of them would sail again.

"Come on, my beauty. Show us what you're made of." He reached for the overhead lever and pulled. The ship's whistle sounded.

WHOOOOOOOOOOOOooooooooo!

Loud and clear, it echoed from mountaintop to mountaintop, and up and down the lake.

"Holy cow! The old man's got her working again. I don't believe it!" Dusty put down his chainsaw and watched in amazement as the *Moyie* whistled, belched smoke from her funnel, and slowly, oh so slowly, was propelled forward by the turning paddle.

123

Dusty scratched his head. "Dunno how he's managed that, but good for him." He watched a few more minutes. "Now that's a pretty sight, real pretty."

He returned to dismembering the tree.

Beneath his feet, Captain Olund felt vibrations as the pistons started to work. The vibrations gradually increased, then he heard it. The sound that had haunted his dreams in retirement. A rhythmic thrashing as each paddle of the giant wheel at the *Moyie's* stern hit the water and came up dripping.

He spoke into the brass tube beside him. "Quarter steam."

"Aye aye, Captain."

The *Moyie* moved purposefully forward, her paddle beating faster. "You're alive again," the captain whispered. He turned the wheel gently. The *Moyie* moved gracefully to one side. He spun it the other way. Once more she responded.

"Half steam."

"Half steam it is, Captain."

The wheel beat faster, churning the water into froth. A wave appeared under the *Moyie's* bow.

"Everything as it should be?" Captain Olund asked.

"She's runnin' as sweet as a mine of molasses!" Boulder hollered back.

Captain Olund sighed with relief. "Full steam ahead then."

"Full steam it is, Sir."

"One more voyage together. One more short voyage." The captain took the helm, unaware of tears of joy sparkling on his cheeks. The *Moyie* obediently thrashed her way through the sunlit waters, towards Mosquito Creek.

Puzzled, Dusty pulled his truck over to the side of the road, rolled down the window, and peered across the lake at the *Moyie*.

"What in heaven's name is the old man up to? The silly old coot's going the wrong way."

He'd kept an eye on the *Moyie* for the last ten minutes, expecting the sternwheeler to head back to Kaslo. It hadn't happened.

"Can't be sailin' on his own," Dusty pondered, chewing his cheek. "There must be at least three of them. Old Boulder for sure. He worked a season on the sternwheelers."

Suddenly his face hardened. He squinted into the distance and focused on a tiny figure on the cargo deck.

Dusty's fist thumped the dash. "That's one of those misbegotten kids—them and old Boulder are helping the captain."

Dusty was furious. He knew where the *Moyie* was heading—Mosquito Creek! He jerked into gear, gunned the engine, and roared down the road in a haze of blue smoke.

"Tarnation…I wasted time pulling down that darned tree. Those little devils might beat me to it!"

Willow ran back to the stokehole before her break had ended. "I think Dusty's caught on!" she shouted above the noise. "He's burning up the highway. We'll never catch him now." Shoulders dropping, she returned to her shovelling.

Melissa looked at Boulder in dismay. "I knew it! We've got to get there first. Tell the captain to go faster."

Boulder shook his head. "Ain't more than one miracle in a day." He patted the *Moyie*'s side affectionately. "The old girl's running, that's miracle enough."

He placed his mouth near the speaking tube. "Coal's low," he warned. Melissa stamped the deck in frustration.

"Mosquito Creek in sight. Half steam," the captain's calm voice floated down.

"Half steam it is, Captain."

"No! NO!" yelled Melissa, grabbing the speaking tube. "Dusty's nearly there. Full steam, full steam!"

"Sorry, lassie. I'm captain."

Boulder gave the sign for the kids to stop shovelling.

Melissa threw up her hands in despair and ran to the bow of the ship, willing it to get there in time.

"Blimey O'Riley...I don't believe it." Dusty slammed on the brakes and squealed to a stop. He looked angrily at the washed-out bridge and the roaring creek eating away at the road.

"Good thing I'm close. This has gotta be the stream before Mosquito Creek. An' I've gotta be on the other side."

Dusty abandoned the truck. Grabbing his chainsaw and backpack from the rear, he headed upstream, pushing through bushes and leaping from rock to rock, looking for a crossing place.

The stately sternwheeler slowly approached the gravel beach.

"Steady, steady, old girl." As he had done a thousand times before, Captain Olund nosed the *Moyie* in, inch by inch, until the gravel bottom held her fast. He slid open the pilothouse window and waved to his crew. "Welcome to Mosquito Creek."

Melissa, Rick, and Willow were already hanging over the side looking for the best place to leap ashore.

Boulder scuttled out onto the deck rubbing his hands. "Nice work, Captain. You ain't lost your touch."

Rick grinned and saluted. "Requesting shore leave, Captain."

"Shore leave granted."

"Quit fooling around," said Melissa angrily. "Dusty may be staking the silver boulder right now!" She jumped in the shallow water and stumbled and splashed her way onto the beach.

The others followed.

Fifty years ago, steam engines powered civilization. They drove railway locomotives and ships, and factories and lumber camps. Cheap and simple to operate, steam engines required only water, fuel, and one skilled operator supported by unskilled workers.

Most sternwheelers used wood as fuel, but the S.S. *Moyie* used coal supplied by railway. The coal was loaded into the stokehold below the foredeck. Stokers threw coal into the firebox, where it burned. The hot gases produced by the fire were drawn through the boiler in many tubes and escaped up the funnel. The water surrounding the tubes boiled, and the resulting steam was taken in pipes to the engines. The *Moyie* had two engines near the stern of the ship that powered the big paddlewheel.

Steam power had its drawbacks. The fire had to burn long enough to heat the water. Faulty boilers or pipes occasionally burst, killing or injuring people in the explosion or scalding them with escaping steam. And unless coal is burned completely, it dirties the air, causing illnesses such as asthma. Today, most engines are powered by diesel fuel or electricity.

www.yesteryeartoys.com/howsteamworks/y101.htm

CHAPTER FIFTEEN

Dusty had beaten them to it. They couldn't see him, but they could hear him bushwhacking through the undergrowth farther up the creek.

Melissa gazed at the scene before her and frowned. The beach was at the head of a small gully running back into the mountain. It was filled with lush vegetation half obscuring thousands of fallen rocks. A mountain stream tumbled between them. "How do we find our boulder among all these?" her voice trembled. "And Dusty's already here."

"Dusty hasn't found the boulder, or he'd be down here boasting," said Willow.

"We're looking for something big," said Rick. "And don't forget that we've got the map."

Melissa fumbled in her purse and pulled it out. Three heads bent over it. Melissa jabbed the map with her finger. "The cross is marked halfway up, beside the stream."

"Quit hanging around then!" Boulder came up behind them and slowly started to pick his way up the side of a small waterfall.

Feeling more cheerful, Melissa, Willow, and Rick soon overtook him and pushed their way upstream.

An hour later, the dreaded confrontation finally took place.

"What's the matter? You experts haven't found the boulder yet?" Dusty jeered from the top of a small rocky cliff. He laughed down at Melissa, Rick, and Willow. "You've got no idea what you're looking for. Never mind, I'll show you when I've staked it."

Dusty disappeared to continue his search farther along Mosquito Creek. The friends could hear him rustling through the forest, and the occasional chink of his pick on rocks.

"He's right." Melissa wiped the sweat from her brow and collapsed on a rock at the base of the cliff. The others followed her example. "I thought a big boulder would be easy to see. But it's not. It's impossible."

Rick nodded glumly. "We've beaten our way up and down this dratted gully three times. The map doesn't work and the haiku obviously isn't a clue, there's no cedar wrapping *anywhere*."

Willow lay on her stomach, dipped her cupped hands into the rushing torrent beside them, and thirstily drank. She wiped her wet hands over her face and neck and sighed.

Answering sighs came from the other two.

The crew looked frightful. Not only were they covered

in coal dust, but they had slipped on rocks, tripped over roots, and snagged their clothes and skin on twigs. They were all at the end of their rope.

Boulder Bob staggered slowly into view. He dropped his pick and kit and lowered himself creakily onto a rock where he could lean against the cliff.

"Boulder, are you sure this is the right place?" Melissa's voice shook.

"Mosquito Creek. That's what Tommy said," Boulder muttered. "But it were a long time ago." He sagged on his seat. "'T'ain't no good. I'm finished, I'm beat." Boulder closed his eyes, suddenly looking as old and wrinkled as an Egyptian mummy.

"Better face it. Grandfather must have got it wrong. There is no silver boulder." Melissa's whole body drooped with disappointment.

"He got the mosquitoes right," said Rick, scratching.

"One good thing, though," said Willow. "Dusty hasn't found it either."

No one bothered answering.

The long silence was complete except for the roar of the swollen creek and Boulder's soft snores.

"Let's check once more." Melissa pulled the diary out of her purse and opened it.

Rick, Willow, and Melissa studied the map.

"The cross is by a wiggle in the creek." Rick pointed. "The only real wiggle I've seen is around the cliff here."

"It's hard to see the whole creek from the ground,"

131

said Willow. "Let's climb up to where Dusty was. Then we can look down on it."

Rick and Willow grasped some sturdy roots and, digging their feet in mossy cracks, swarmed up the small cliff.

Rick hooked his arm around a cedar tree growing on top and hung over the edge. "Yup. This *is* the only wiggle," he called.

"Hard to tell without the map," argued Willow. She lay down and hung over the cliff, her arm outstretched. "Pass it up, Melissa, so we can check."

By stretching on her tiptoes, Melissa could just reach Willow's fingers. She passed over the diary.

Rick and Willow held it out, orienting it to the angle of the creek.

"Hey!" Willow shouted suddenly. "What if the creek bed has changed?"

Melissa groaned. "Then the boulder could be anywhere. We'll *never* find it."

"Watch out!" Rick sounded the alarm. "I hear Dusty heading this way again."

Willow dropped the diary back down to Melissa. "Hide the map," she whispered.

Rick sat on the edge of the cliff and tobogganed down to the ground. Willow followed.

"Thanks a lot, you guys," said Melissa angrily as debris rained down on her and Boulder Bob.

She blinked and rubbed her face. "Now I've got dirt in my eyes."

Boulder woke with a start and looked up at the cliff. He started to laugh.

Melissa turned on him. "It's not funny."

Boulder wheezed and cackled. "It's funny, all right," he croaked, pointing to the cliff with a shaky hand.

Rick and Willow had torn away moss and small roots when they slid down. The exposed rock gleamed a dull silver.

"This is it?" Melissa gasped. "This is the boulder? It's gigantic!"

Everyone stared in wonder.

"But it's not a boulder—it's a cliff," said Willow.

"I reckon it was a boulder. I reckon a small avalanche filled in behind it," said Boulder Bob. "So it ain't standing on its own no more."

Willow leapt forward and pulled away more roots. "Look. The haiku…it *is* a clue. 'Cedar-wrapped rock, earth gift.' That's the part we didn't understand. It's the cedar tree on top. Its roots are wrapped around the boulder!"

With trembling hands, Melissa unfolded the paper. She read softly, "Moonlight, gift from sky. Cedar-wrapped rock, gift from earth. Each reflecting each."

Melissa gently stroked the shining surface. "Grandfather must have found it in the evening. It would be beautiful in the moonlight. 'Each reflecting each,'" she quoted again.

Boulder blew his nose loudly. "Reflection Creek, that's what Tommy called it. Reflection Creek."

"Quick. Get staking. Dusty's almost here," Rick interrupted.

133

Melissa touched Boulder's arm. "You first," she said. "For you and Tommy." She pulled a metal stake from her purse.

Boulder took the stake and walked down the creek bed, followed by the others. He cleared a space for the stake in the bank.

"Quick. Hammer it in." Rick handed over the old man's pick.

Clunk, clunk, clunk. The downstream stake stood firmly.

Boulder paced upstream along the edge of the creek and pointed between his feet. "You do the other one, right here." He passed Melissa his pick.

Melissa nodded and rapidly drove in a stake.

Manic laughter interrupted them. Dusty erupted from the bushes, where he'd been spying.

"Gotcha... gotcha, gotcha, got cha!" Dusty chanted. "Thanks for finding the silver boulder for me." He pointed to Boulder. "He can't stake. He hasn't had a permit for years."

"Permit! Permit?" Boulder yelled, completely losing his temper. "Who needs a permit, you young pup? I bin staking long before you or your daddy was born." He clenched his fists and lunged forward.

Rick and Willow moved in to stop him. Each grabbed an arm and hung on.

"No! NO!" Willow yelled. "Remember what happened when you hit Meddlesome."

134

The old man sagged suddenly and sat on a fallen tree trunk. Willow and Rick stood behind him, glaring at Dusty.

"Exactly," Dusty grinned, still standing his ground. He fished in his pocket. "You're way out of date, old man. Now me, I've got the permit *and* the numbered stakes." He dangled a piece of paper in front of them.

Melissa stepped forward. "Thank you for informing us of the procedure," she said icily. "But these stakes are mine. They *are* numbered correctly and I think you'll find my permit is all in order."

She reached in her bag and pulled out a matching form.

"Well, I'll be darned," said Boulder. "Everything above board. Just like her grandfather."

Willow, Rick, and Boulder let rip an earsplitting whoop. An answering whistle came from the *Moyie*.

White-faced, Dusty Malone stared at Boulder. "After all these years...You and a bunch of kids have found the silver boulder." He turned on Melissa. "Who the heck are you, anyway?"

Melissa answered him proudly. "I'm Tommy's grand-daughter. *My* grandfather found this boulder. *Your* grand-father tried to steal it. Are you going to do the same?"

"Atta girl." Boulder chuckled, making a mock punch in Dusty's direction.

Dusty stepped backwards, his hands up in surrender. "Hey, hey, who said anything about stealing? Not me."

No one answered.

"Okay…okay…so a bunch of city pups and an old murderer got lucky. What a world!" Dusty tucked his permit in his pocket and turned to go.

Suddenly he changed his mind and spun around again. "Tell me, Miss high and mighty Tommy's granddaughter, are those your only stakes?"

Melissa nodded.

Dusty sneered at her. "Then I'm going to do some real prospecting. I'll find the vein that troublesome boulder came from." He pushed his way past them and headed up the creek. His voice floated back derisively. "Think that boulder's rich? You ain't seen nothing yet."

A week later, Rick, Willow, and Melissa were lying on Kaslo Beach, sipping pops and watching construction workers put the finishing touches on the *Moyie*'s cradle.

While the lake was still in flood, the *Moyie* had been towed back and floated over the cradle. Then crews worked for twenty-four hours, as the waters receded, rebuilding and readjusting as she settled.

"I was terrified during the storm," said Melissa. "But it was amazing to sail to Mosquito Creek in the *Moyie*. This holiday has been the most exciting time of my whole life."

"Us too," Rick agreed.

"It was so moving when the band played on Front Street as the *Moyie* was towed back. It was like being in one of Boulder Bob's stories."

 When a prospector finds a deposit of valuable minerals, he or she needs to safeguard the discovery. The government allows a prospector to "stake a claim"—to reserve a piece of land around the find so it can be explored and developed without having to fight off other prospectors.

Modern prospectors must purchase a licence from the government and are given a set of metal tags to attach to wooden posts marking the boundaries of the claim. Then they must register the location of the claim at a Mining Recorder's office.

Once a claim is staked, the finder may develop it or sell it to someone else. Smart prospectors rush to stake a claim where others have been made. An Alberta prospector once found a 12-foot (4-metre) strip between two claims that had not been staked. He made a fortune there, and was known ever afterwards as "Twelve-Foot Davis."

www.bc-mining-house.com/prospecting_school/ep_claim.htm (to find out how to stake your own claim in B.C.—when you're eighteen)
http://sciencenorth.on.ca/groundwork/CIMeng/gwintro.htm (to play a mine discovery game)

"Finding the silver boulder *is* one of his stories. And it's getting better every time he tells it," laughed Willow.

"And I'll never forget being in the documentary your mom and dad are making." Melissa struck a dramatic pose. "Me...a film star."

Willow chuckled again. "*I'll* never forget the shock on Mom and Dad's faces when they realized it was us on board the *Moyie*. I thought Dad would drop the camera in the lake."

"Yeah, it was lucky they got back from Nelson just as the town was sending out boats to locate the *Moyie*," said Rick. "If they'd gone straight to the bus and found it empty, they would have flipped. They just shipped aboard to film the rescue, thinking we were safely with you."

"You *were* with me," Melissa grinned. "Safely *adrift*."

Everyone laughed.

"What's going to happen to the boulder?" Rick asked.

"One of my uncles is setting up a company for me and Boulder Bob. The silver boulder will be melted down." Melissa rolled onto her side and looked seriously at Rick and Willow. "You realize I'll be giving you some shares."

"Shares?" said Rick. "Sharing what?"

Melissa laughed. "Shares in the company, so that when we sell the lead and silver, you get some money. The boulder's been assayed. It's going to be worth a chunk of cash."

"Actually, I'd rather have a chunk off the boulder for my mineral collection...but a mountain bike would be good, too."

Melissa laughed and laughed. "You're as bad as Boulder Bob and the captain. They're donating some of their shares to the *Moyie*."

Willow stood up and shook the sand out of her towel. "You guys coming?"

"Where?" asked Melissa.

"To the Langham. I want to log on to the Net."

"What for?" asked Rick. "We finished our correspondence lessons for the day."

"To check out silver prices on the stock market, dummy. If I'm getting shares, I'm going to learn about investing!"

AUTHORS' NOTE

This story is a work of fiction but it's set against a real background. We have been visiting the towns of Kaslo and Sandon for years, and we like to imagine the historic buildings as they were in their early days. The Langham Building still stands in Kaslo and is the scene of an arts festival every summer, so we were able to use its past and present life in our story. The nineteenth-century Kaslo flood really took place, and we have often wondered what would happen if there were to be another one now.

The *Moyie* is one of the last existing sternwheelers in the world. She is beached in Kaslo and is a museum. One of the *Moyie's* curators of the museum lived on board for a while. We interviewed one of her captains, who told us the "green meat" story.

Sandon was indeed founded on the discovery of a silver boulder, and later the town was preserved for many years by an elderly man who lived there alone. The Japanese character Tomi (Tommy) is fictional but the Japanese internment story is all too authentic. The

Nikkei Internment Centre in New Denver and the exhibit in the Langham make it possible for visitors to see how Japanese Canadians had to live during the war years.

Although some of our characters are rooted in history and the places are real, this is a totally fictitious story. None of our characters exist, and none of these events took place. However, the rivalry for a precious find that we tell about in this story has parallels in many of the old mining stories.

Watch for further adventures of Rick and Willow as they become involved in an Alberta dinosaur dig.

—*Andrea and David Spalding*

ABOUT THE AUTHORS

Andrea and David Spalding live on Pender Island, British Columbia. They spent many years performing stories and folk music in Canadian schools, and are now full-time writers. Their children are grown, giving them freedom to travel across Canada and write about their discoveries.

Andrea has written eight books for children, including *Finders Keepers, An Island of My Own, Phoebe and the Gypsy, Sarah May and the New Red Dress,* and *Me and Mr. Mah.* Her books for adults include biographies, cookbooks, and guidebooks.

David has written, co-written, or edited ten books. Most are about science for adults, with recent books on dinosaurs and whales. He has also written short stories and radio programs and contributed to encyclopedias and textbooks.

For more information about the Spaldings, check out their Web site at www.gulfislands.com/spalding/. Readers are welcome to contact the authors at andreas@gulfislands.com or at Whitecap Books, 351 Lynn Avenue, North Vancouver, BC, V7J 2C4.